Penny
Tyas

Acres of Light

Acres of Light

Everybody has secrets

Sou Tyas

The best sister anyone could have.
The world is a poorer place
without you in it

My thanks go to Jan Smith and Nicola Hok for their constant support and enthusiasm to help make my Wish come true. To my niece Gemma who showed me how to be a grown-up, and to my family and friends who heard me talk about wanting to become a writer for ten years, and read numerous drafts, before arriving at this point. Any errors in this work of fiction are mine, not theirs.

About the Author

Penny Tyas was born in England but spent many years sailing and living in the Caribbean. She returned to England in 2009 and has since been diagnosed with Multiple Sclerosis. Forever the optimist, she has turned away from the things she can no longer do, and started a new career doing what she loves – creative writing. She is currently studying for a degree in history, and lives in Hampshire with her son and a cat. This is her first novel.

TABLE OF CONTENTS

PROLOGUE

Icy black rain was falling, the pavement's gentle slope creating rivers down the high street. Although it was not long after lunch, the sky was dark and forbidding. Cars travelled slowly, their headlights on, reflecting off the wet road. Visibility was so distorted by the heavy rain, even the lighted shop windows of the high street were pale and indistinct as if the rain had washed all the colour from the world.

People hurried along the pavement in coats and hats and under dark umbrellas pulled so low they could only see their own feet. Headless dark shadows jostling in all directions.

As the cars paraded slowly down the high street, a bicycle pulled out from a side street. The rider was almost completely obscured by the red Musto jacket - hood up, swathed in scarves so only the eyes were visible. At that precise moment, a huge gust of wind funnelled down between tall buildings along the street. A table outside a coffee shop was blown over and rolled into the road.

Warning shouts, a scream, sudden flashes of red light, squealing brakes, skidding tyres, a sickening thud, breaking glass, grinding metal, then … silence. Time stopped for a matter of seconds. A broken bicycle wheel rolled down the road before it lost its momentum and collapsed. Silence. The whole place holding its breath ...

Chapter 1 - First Class

Acres of Light

Jessica had thought long and hard about what to wear, and even as she was deciding on the matching underwear and flat shoes, she recognised how ludicrous she was being. Nobody in the art class was going to get to see her underwear! This was her first time as a life drawing model, and she was nervous.

Jessica caught the bus which stopped right outside the Horton Regis Community Centre and went through the double doors into reception. There were all sorts of people milling around; little girls in buns and tutus right up to grannies attending any of the U3A classes on offer. The receptionist was busy, so being mindful of the time she looked around for inspiration. She watched an older gentleman struggle through the double doors carrying two heavy looking bags and trying to keep hold of an artist palette that kept slipping from under his arm.

"Excuse me" said Jessica "are you here for the art class? I'm not sure where to go."

"Oh, no problem, just follow me then" he said.

Jessica relieved him of the palette and followed him up the stairs.

"Are you a new student?" he asked. "I don't think I was expecting anyone else this term."

"Actually I'm the model" said Jessica.

"Oh my dear! I'm so sorry, I have led you astray!" he laughed, and Jessica looked perplexed.

"I teach a watercolour class" he explained "you need the life drawing which is on the other side of the building!" He gave her directions. She retraced her steps down the stairs, along the corridor, past the coffee shop and the table covered with second-hand books for sale, up another two flights of stairs before arriving at her destination. She was a little frustrated; she had envisioned arriving cool and composed. Now she approached the door late, puffing, and red in the face.

There is something rather wondrous about stepping through the door from a gloomy grim Community Centre corridor into the light of a studio. The smell of linseed oil and pencil shavings, and light. Acres of light. Not artificially produced from argon and lithium but streaming through the glass ceiling from the whole universe above.

The walls were covered in an assortment of notices; what to do in the case of a fire, instructions on keeping the studio clean for others. Several boards showed artwork from other classes. Some were obviously life drawings, others still life or landscapes. It was a relief to see that the life drawings didn't include facial portraits. Even if she ended up on the wall, she could still be anonymous. There were about a dozen nervous looking students in the room, all much older than herself, and a rather scruffy man who seemed to be in charge. He acknowledged Jessica coldly, unaware or uninterested

4

in her name, which just added to her discomfort on this foreign stage.

"Right then, now that our model has finally arrived, we can get down to some real work. My name is Patrick and I am your tutor for the next 12 weeks. Although this is not a certificated course, it is nonetheless worthy of being treated as such. I do expect you all to attend every class and not use it as a way to fill-in on an otherwise uneventful Thursday morning. My time is valuable and I don't intend to squander it going over things you have omitted to pay attention to."

Patrick had the look of an artist; his fingers permanently stained with charcoal, flecks of blue and white paint in his hair from a project already set aside. The odious adage "Those who can, do - those who can't, teach" niggled at the back of his subconscious and made him negative, critical and bitter, yet his enthusiasm for what his pupils might achieve with the right direction made him a better than average tutor.

Patrick really couldn't be doing with models, they thought too highly of themselves with all the attention they were given. He truly believed that sitting about for hours with all eyes focussed on them made them arrogant – "look at me – I'm the talent" – they were merely a prop – no more and no less than a bowl of fruit. The artists would always be the talent in the room. In his world Art was something that you learned and practiced. It took up more than three hours a week in a class of mature students, in a cramped studio with the under 11's ballet class banging around down the hallway.

As he spoke, Patrick walked around the perimeter adjusting blinds and windows for the perfect stage setting, finding cushions and stools for Jessica to use and positioning the podium on its castors in the centre of the room.

JESSICA

In the far corner Patrick had set up a folding wooden screen and indicated Jessica should go behind to undress. Sweat was running down her temple, and even though she had showered before coming here, she still noticed her own smell when taking off her bra - a musty musky smell emanating from under pendulous breasts. Screen or no screen, she had never felt so embarrassed and ashamed. She couldn't even remember why she had agreed to this; getting paid to take off her clothes just felt like the act of a whore. She wanted to run away but couldn't bear the embarrassment of leaving in front of all those artists.

Once Jessica was completely naked, devoid of even her watch and glasses, she draped a robe around herself and stepped back into the light of the studio. Patrick motioned for her to take up position, and carefully placing her robe over the back of a chair Jessica walked up onto the podium hoping that her cheeks were not as red as they felt.

Looking around at the artists, some of the women gave her an encouraging smile, but mainly they were ignoring her, and the three men present would not even look her in the eye. She had thought that being stared at would be the embarrassing part, but this complete disregard was even worse. As directed, she took up a foetal position in the centre of the podium.

Patrick threw a large sheet of paper on the floor where he knelt and brushed the page with a piece of charcoal cupped between his fingers. "We might call this class Life Drawing, but it is more than just *drawing*, it is *feeling*" Jessica felt uncomfortable watching Patrick caress the paper whilst keeping his eyes firmly on her. It was rather sexual and revolting, with the artists as voyeurs. "I want you to feel the picture with your hands. Be free to show how the person appears as you bring it forth from the paper, our bodies do not have black outlines, we have shadows and dark places, see where the light hits the skin. ... Let your picture grow"

From her foetal position, it was a little hard to see what had been drawn, but to Jessica it just looked like a gigantic ink blot. She felt rather disappointed and tried to focus her attention elsewhere. She could just make out part of the studio wall where some artwork was displayed; a wild rugged landscape, perhaps the Scottish Highlands? Perhaps the boulder in the foreground was hiding the English Redcoats? perhaps the Jacobites were forming an attack from the distant crag? Perhaps she wouldn't do this again.

Patrick stood and moved around the class "I want you all to work without trying to define lines and forms, but to mould what you see – all the light and shadows and dark places." A sense of excitement - a pending anticipation, as huge sheets of new paper are pulled out of the pile with a great whoosh and pinned up on easels - blank pages ready to become works of art. Absent of conversation the only sounds were of pencils being sharpened, easels scraping on the floor to gain the perfect view, the tinkle of brushes in jars of water, removing the evidence of older projects in order to start anew.

Following Patrick's direction, Jessica re-positioned herself into a more comfortable semi-prone pose. Now able to see a little more of the group, her mood changed. It became apparent that she was not insignificant or something to be ignored. This was not embarrassing, it was embracing. The students looked at her not with revulsion as she had feared, but as something complex and interesting. Their concentration was entirely on her form – she was a challenge, and the struggle was within the artists themselves. It had become easier for Jessica to relax and accept that she had a proper role to play in this class – simply by keeping still she was assisting the artists to be the best they could be.

Amidst the shushing sounds of rubbing charcoal on paper, Patrick's was the only voice to be heard as he continued to move between the easels.

"No. You see you have given her an outline that doesn't exist..... You need to be freer with your hands.... No! No! No! – you have not been listening"

It seemed that each of the artists needed a little word of criticism. Patrick was letting them know that they were wrong and he was right. No one seemed to question that his idea of right was an unrecognisable smudge on a page.

THE CLASS

Patrick directed Jessica to change pose again, so she made a compromise between comfort and contortion and settled back to watch the artists watching her.

The artists were mainly women, and although she didn't know them, Jessica could tell a lot from just watching their body language. Whispering, shrugs, looks of confusion all indicating their nervousness, nobody quite at home yet in this new environment.

Directly in her line of sight was a woman with spiky white hair. She wore an artist's smock which, like Patrick's, showed the stains and blotches of previous projects. Painfully thin, her cheeks were sunken, and shadows formed around her eyes. She didn't look strong enough to manage all the bags and artist paraphernalia she had around her. Jessica suspected the gentleman who was hovering at her elbow had helped her bring it all in and was possibly her husband. He seemed very charming, smiling at everyone and introducing himself in whispers as Martin and being attentive to his wife, but she in turn was very dismissive and cold What was that all about thought Jessica. Next to her was a blond woman, probably in her early forties but still showing traces of the beauty she once was. Her hair pulled back into a perfect French pleat, her nails perfectly shaped. She had made more of an effort with her appearance than her neighbour. Although she wore jeans and a T shirt, like everything else about her, they were perfect; perfectly pressed, perfectly clean. Her working area was perfectly organized; charcoal and paints neatly arranged in rows, paintbrushes in a Happy Mother's Day Mug. She had a tea towel thrown over one shoulder like professional chefs do, to wipe hands, mop up spills etc., but her clothes were dangerously unprotected. Too perfect thought Jessica. She felt sure they wouldn't be perfectly clean by the end of the session!

An elderly gentleman had set himself up at the station closest to the door. He looked nervous and uncomfortable; Jessica wasn't sure if it was her nudity or Patrick's high-handedness that was to blame. She noticed his working area was very minimalist as though he was poised to make a quick exit. Three grey haired ladies arranged their easels close to each other and were obviously old acquaintances. They kept themselves to themselves, conferring with each other in whispers, reminding Jessica of the three witches in Macbeth. The remaining half dozen students looked like real novices. Keen faces ready with pencils sharpened and virgin sketch pads, eager to learn a new skill and prepared to do everything Patrick asked of them.

As before, Patrick directed how she should position herself, letting the students know this would be a longer pose. To keep her head from moving, Jessica chose a point on the floor to stare at. Dirty blue linoleum with random blobs of dried paint and ink. She tried to make images out of them just as she used to do with clouds on a sunny day. Lying on the grass staring at the sky … that one looks like a dog begging for treats, a castle ruins, a huge baby's head. It would have been much more fun as a game if played with someone else - can they see what I see? Just like then, there was no-one here to share the game with. Without her glasses on, the blobs before her eyes started to move and merge, fading out of focus. She wanted to close her eyes and drift away.

"Coffee break everyone." Patrick's voice brought Jessica's consciousness back into the room. "Back here ready to start again in thirty minutes."

As the class put down their charcoal and brushes there was a general hum of conversation, a picking up of handbags and a move towards the exit. Patrick had been first to leave, and Jessica was left without direction, not knowing if she was invited to join the others, not wanting to go out in just her robe, and feeling silly about getting dressed and undressed all over again. As she was just sitting there feeling very naked and lost, Martin poked his head back round the door. "I'm sorry, that was rude of me, can I bring you a

11

coffee or something?" - it was a nice gesture and she asked for a glass of water, but it made her feel very exposed. She didn't want to be caught out like that again, so she got up, put on her robe, and went to have a secret look at what the artists had accomplished.

JESSICA WAITING

Jessica was 26, a grown-up; an age when she could have been married, bringing up kids, running a household, having a career. None of these labels fitted her though. Here she was sitting naked in a room of strangers. What kind of career is that? she thought. She was not the smartest person around. At school she had at various times been labelled as having dyspraxia, dyslexia, and dyscalculia. Jessica wasn't stupid, but the synapses in her brain seemed to run at a slower pace than everyone else's. If her contemporaries were on Wi-Fi, she was still on dial-up. She was also not the skinniest person around. Years of comfort eating had put enough padding on her to be edging upwards of dress size 18. According to BMI data on diet websites that labelled her as morbidly obese.

Being intellectually a little slow and physically a lot overweight had meant a torturous journey through school. Years of bullying and embarrassment leading to a total loss of confidence in herself. In fact she had a really pretty face and wondrously shiny hair; if she took a little more trouble with her appearance it could have made all the difference to her self-esteem. Instead she hardly ever bothered with moisturiser and make-up, and kept her hair tied back with an unimaginative scrunchy. The artists, however, could see her beauty;

could see life in her curves, warmth in her face and her hair, when freed from its scrunchy, fell down round her shoulders like a mahogany waterfall.

Jessica didn't really know what to expect when she peeked at the art, and was surprised by the diverse styles and skills of the artists. Some pieces she obviously admired more than others, particularly the quick sketches with not much detail. One in particular stood out to her. It was a charcoal sketch, not showing a head or even feet and hands, but although it was anonymous to anyone else, Jessica was astounded at how the artist had captured the curve of her buttocks, the crease by her belly button, the shape of her neck. The size of her thighs and tummy and breasts had been captured precisely, but not in a grotesque way, not a caricature. Everything about it was beautiful yet at the same time it was her. Never before had she put those two ideas in the same sentence. She had never once thought of her body as beautiful, yet the artist had portrayed her exactly and still it was beauty.

COMMUNITY COFFEE

The little cafe at the Community Centre was from an era way before the smart coffee houses on the High Street. Here they joyfully served instant coffee, tap water without ice, or a pot of tea for one. The array of homemade cakes, however, surpassed the plastic

14

wrapped confections from the franchised fashionable places and made up for the shortcomings on the drinks.

The three witches settled themselves around a corner table and continued whatever line of gossip had kept them enthralled whilst in class. They appeared self-contained without any need to enlarge their circle of acquaintances. The rest of the class, however, sat at the long centre table, each voice adding another layer to the introductions and friendly enquiries.

Martin carried a tray to the table and sat next to the spiky haired lady, bringing her tea and cake. She continued to be dismissive of her husband, and so as not to seem disheartened by this, he started chatting to the rather attractive blonde opposite him.

"Hello, I'm Martin, and this is my wife Fiona. Perhaps I should not be sitting here with all you talented lot, I have no natural ability myself. I am only here to help out" Martin was in his early sixties, casually but neatly dressed. His whole manner was obsequious; smooth and well-rehearsed.

"I'm Caroline, and I am sure we're all delighted to have you join us."

"Well that's very gracious. Have you been doing this long?"

"Not really, I have dabbled a bit in oils in the past, but this is my first life drawing class. How about you? You say you have no talent, but have you even tried?"

"Not at all - I leave the creativity in our family to my wife. She is quite a dedicated painter, no time for

15

anything else really so it would be overkill for me to get in the way of such talent."

"So what do you do?"

"I'm in insurance!" he said with such pride that Caroline regretted asking the question as soon as it was out of her mouth. Apparently insurance and actuarial tables could keep Martin enthralled for the whole of the coffee break.

The small talk continued as this group of strangers took the first steps to being classmates; introductions, likes and dislikes, life stories. Caroline tried to join in but it was hard to concentrate with Martin jabbering on about over 50's life cover and the importance of covering funeral costs.

SECOND SESSION

The second session began when everyone returned from their break. Martin brought Jessica the glass of water she had asked for, and a piece of Dorset Apple cake that she had not. She was already positioned on the podium, taking off her robe and using it to sit on as the carpet tiles on the podium made it feel like sitting on a dish scrubber. Jessica declined the cake, not wishing to be seen as an obese stark-naked woman shoving cake down her throat, but managed a few sips of water before Patrick made a grand entrance barking out orders before the door had even closed behind him.

"Right, this time we will go for an even longer pose." He fetched cushions, giving them to Jessica to use on the podium "Use the pillows to make a comfortable position, semi reclining. Not so comfortable that you will fall asleep, remember the artists are paying you, so try to be something worth studying."

This time Jessica settled into position with her head propped on her hand, as if she were on a couch watching television. She was now facing the window and focused on the roof line and chimney at the far end of the community centre. The sky was a pale blue wash with the slate tiles on the roof picked out clearly. A couple of tiles needed replacing, slipping down from the symmetry of the rows above and below. The next winter storm would probably see them fall. She could hear the traffic below, and a fire engine siren in the distance. It was as if, by focusing on the scene outside, she had left the studio and her mind could wander away.

A couple of times she asked permission to move as parts of her body fell asleep and went numb. The arm holding up her head went numb a few times and she was able to remove it from the couch, straighten it, shake the hand and wiggle the fingers without disturbing the rest of her pose at all. When her foot began to cramp up, Patrick allowed her to get up and move around. He put chalk marks on the podium and pillows around her to mark the position she needed to return to. Jessica took the opportunity for a bathroom break and put her robe back on, padding barefoot out the door and down the corridor. She used the disabled toilet so nobody would hear her, and sat on the toilet stamping her foot on the floor, flexing and shaking it until normal blood flow resumed and the blue grey tinge returned to pale pink. Jessica padded back to the studio and took up position again, hoping it was not going to be for much longer.

Finally the first class was over, Jessica uncoiled herself and stretched out her screaming muscles. The artists thanked her, Patrick paid her and left, and Jessica went back behind the screen to get dressed.

The level of conversation rose as people who had been strangers at the beginning of the class were now conversing and comparing. New links founded in a commonality of experience. Snatches of conversation drifted behind the screen.

"Oh that's a very good start - I like your ..."

"That's impressive. I take it blue is ..."

" ... will you continue with it ..."

Jessica didn't want to interrupt the spontaneity of opinions, but she also didn't want the embarrassment of overhearing anything personal about herself, so she fixed a smile on her face and emerged from behind the screen.

Everyone turned to look at her, surprised that she was still in the room. The silence that hung in the air was growing. She felt more exposed now than when she was naked, and wanted to explain that she hadn't been eavesdropping, but courage failed her and she remained standing, unsure of her next move. After what felt like an eternity, the spiky haired woman invited her to join them all in viewing their output. Jessica felt a sense of inclusion burst over her like sunshine.

The artist who had done the quick sketch she had so admired before, now apologised for his work.

"I'm sorry - it's not very flattering."

"No, I think it's great - it is definitely me."

"I prefer just doing quick sketches - I get bored filling in detail"

"I like sketches …"

Jessica moved towards another easel - this one, instead of charcoal, was in great sweeping arcs of blue, the differing shades bringing out the body in three dimensions.

"This is beautiful …"

"It's not finished yet. This is only the sky." Seeing Jessica looking confused, Fiona explained further " … I turn the painting into a landscape - the life model becomes the undulating hills or clouds."

Jessica just smiled and said nothing. *Is that offensive?* she thought, caught between disappointment that her body was to be so used, and interest to see what the end result would be.

As she went between the easels she could see different levels of expertise and detail. Some easels were already empty - the artist not wishing to have their work viewed, especially by the subject herself. For Jessica, it was an odd feeling to be viewing pictures of her own naked body, whilst currently being fully clothed. The group started to split apart, like the opening shot in a game of pool, each going to pick up their possessions, clean brushes, mop up spills, pack up easels. The moment of inclusion had passed.

Once everyone had left Jessica set off towards the bus station. It had started to rain - the blue sky of the morning turning into grey gloom. Rain running down the shop windows looked as if all colour were being washed away. She managed to catch her bus just as it was about to leave the depot. She went upstairs and sat near the back, private but not alone, wearing a secret smile.

If anyone noticed or cared, they might have thought that it was because she hadn't missed her bus and have to wait the extra hour for the next one, but her smile was more personal - her personal achievement. Not a raging furnace of passion, nor a bubbling cauldron of excitement, but the first instant when kindling is touched by flame - embers that glow bright when they are blown upon. She might be fat, she might be shy, but she had triumphed today in a way she hadn't really expected, and this was enough for now.

CHAPTER 3 - SECOND CLASS

NEWBIES

When Jessica arrived at the studio on the following Thursday morning there was a stranger perched on a stool gazing out the window. He didn't hear her come in and looked completely lost in thought as if something he was staring at in the middle distance would give him answers. Jessica had intended to go straight behind the screen to get ready, but that was not an option with a strange man in the room. She stopped in her tracks, unsure how to proceed then coughed softly.

The man snapped out of his reverie looking surprised. He was tall and muscular and when he turned towards her, Jessica could see the tanned and ruddy complexion of someone who had spent their whole life outdoors.

"Hello? Are you here for the Life Drawing Class?" he said.

"Eh … Yes"

"Well, welcome. Feel free to set up wherever you want" He smiled and gestured at the empty room.

"Actually I'm the model." Said Jessica.

"Brilliant!" he smiled and got down rather clumsily from his perch by the window. As he came towards her, Jessica noticed he walked with a stick and he dragged his left foot a bit. She could see pain in his eyes, even as he tried to hide it.

"I'm Nick, the new tutor; Patrick had to leave suddenly and I'm his replacement." He smiled again and held out his hand. "You must be Jessica. Very pleased to meet you." he said, shaking her hand. He had a warm smile and was such a welcoming personality it was like a breath of fresh air after Patrick, and she immediately felt comfortable in his company. She took herself off behind the screen to get ready as the artists themselves started to arrive.

The same sounds of setting up; easels scraping across the lino and great whooshes as large sheets of paper were pulled from the stack. Unlike last time, there was more animated conversation as people reconnected.

When Jessica came out into the room wearing her robe she noted familiar faces, the absence of some, and a new arrival. She also noted the absence of the odious podium with its scratchy surface. Instead, there was an old armchair draped with swathes of material.

Nick addressed the class "Good morning everyone, my name is Nick and I have been sent by the college to be your new tutor."

There was a bubble of murmured voices and questioning glances.

"Patrick needed to leave suddenly and I have been sent as his stand in."

"Will Patrick be back next week?" someone asked.

"We don't quite know yet, so I will start anew and presume we will all be together for the duration" he continued "it would help me enormously if we could go round and everyone give me your names."

As they went round the class, Jessica also put names to faces she remembered from the previous week; the rather thin woman with spiky white hair was Fiona, next to her the blond woman was called Caroline, and next to Caroline was a new girl called Anthea. It was nice to feel Nick was treating them all as people, not just objects. She felt that Patrick leaving was a good thing - all that feel and grow charcoal blob stuff would be discarded now - it was a relief.

Nick turned to Jessica. "Now - how do you feel about rope?"

NICK

Nick was a career soldier, or had been. Back in Aldershot, the troops were getting ready to deploy to Afghanistan. It was a stressful time for everyone. The women thought about danger, boredom and loneliness, the men thought about danger, adventure and logistics. Wives resented the army for taking up so much of the few precious remaining days in briefings, kit muster, medical checks, shots, late night drinking sessions, camaraderie and war stories. Husbands resented the wives for all the additional pressure they were putting them under just because they were doing their job. "You knew what you signed up for" became the standard phrase between husband and wife.

One of the younger men on base, Rifleman Archer, had a broken leg and couldn't join the rest of his troop when they deployed to Afghan. He was gutted; this would have been his first deployment, his first campaign medal. By the time he was out of rehab, the rest would be on their way back. Jenny and the other wives promised their husbands they would watch out for Archer. Jenny was good like that, she understood what being an army wife involved.

Tensions ran high with all the families right up to the day of departure Resentments were forgotten, love and promises given, brave faces as families split apart as if magnets of the same polarity had been dropped in their midst - a force stronger than themselves pushing each other away.

The first week in Afghanistan was spent at Camp Bastion so the soldiers could acclimatize themselves to extremes of temperature where in summer it could reach 55C and in winter it would freeze. The Army base was home to upwards of twenty thousand people; a city in the sand that never sleeps. Planes and helicopters flew in and out all night; transporting troops, bringing mail and packages from home, moving supplies and men to smaller outlying patrol bases. The facilities on base were impressive; a water plant produced a million litres of fresh water every week, and even made the plastic bottles on-site. A British Forces Broadcasting Service (BFBS) radio station, hospital and trauma unit, gyms, training areas, even a Pizza Hut. It could be a very social place, but it could also get very boring. After a week Nick and the others were deployed to a patrol base deeper inside Helmand and the adrenalin went up a notch.

Nick was woken up shortly after 3am to go on standing guard (stag). He was stiff and cold. The clear vast expanse of sky in Helmand turning the furnace of day into arctic night. His feet were numb from cold and his hands numb where he had slept on them. He kept flicking his hands to get the blood flowing and the feeling back. As usual when on a patrol, he slept with his socks turned inside out in the bottom of his sleeping bag. It kept them warm and dry, which just about made up for the terrible smell. After donning his combat jacket he grabbed an energy bar from his ration pack and dragged on his boots to keep the heat in his feet. He rolled his gear up and sorted his bug-out bag - rule one on guard duty, always be ready for contact.

Nick grabbed his weapon, webbing and a bottle of water from the stash and headed out to spend another few hours staring into darkness, imagining shapes moving in the gloom, slipping between fear and boredom every few minutes. Nick liked the combination of comradeship and solitude on stag; knowing there was someone to cover you, but a beautiful silence at the same time.

The days at Patrol Base were a cacophony of sound - people conducting ordinary lives within the confines of a highly fortified oasis; doing laundry, connecting with home, movies, football, gyms and everything else one does on any Army base in the UK. The difference being here it was hot as hell and you are surrounded by people wanting to kill you.

Going on patrol was a relief in a weird way. The men became self-contained and focussed. There was less chat about home life, emotions, problems. There was not enough brain space left to contemplate those things - except on stag.

Was it his imagination, or had letters from Jenny become less frequent? Was he imagining that Archer was mentioned in every single one? Were the endless tales of coffee with Archer and the girls, ladies' night mess dinners, and other social outings anything he needed to worry about?

He was flicking his right hand again to try and get the blood moving and feeling back, so didn't have a hand on his weapon when he felt a puff of wind speed past his left ear and heard the simultaneous crack of a rifle and thud of a bullet as it hit the tree behind him.

MARTIN

Martin was busying himself clearing up his wife's station and trying not to look at Jessica. He had never been attracted to overweight women, finding all the wobbly bits rather disgusting and he was embarrassed to have her still in the same room but fully clothed. She looked quite normal within the confines of jeans and tee shirt, and she had a pretty face, but all he could see in his mind's eye was the unbridled stomach hanging

26

down to her groin and pendulous breasts like over-filled water balloons sagging down to her knees. He preferred a fit body, full of vitality, a smooth uninterrupted sweep of warm skin, buttocks that fit his hands, breasts that needed no outside support, a body that quivered to his touch, a woman that arched her back in wanting. Fiona used to be such a woman, he had loved her once.

Fiona had been a virgin when they married - he thought that was rather romantic and old-fashioned; he liked the idea of being the first, the one and only. It appealed to his sense of dominance. Martin adored sex in all its forms; making love, lust, highly charged passionate quickies, role playing and kinky fantasies - he loved it all. What had seemed romantic and sweetly innocent on his wedding night however, turned to frustration when it became apparent after a few short months that sex was not as appealing to Fiona as it was to him. She seemed to enjoy the making love part, but would baulk at anything more adventurous. Within a year, Fiona allowed him to have intercourse just a couple of times a month. Even then it was not exactly spontaneous, what with her insistence on condoms and spermicides; was it any wonder that he sought sexual satisfaction outside the marital bed? He was only human after all! Now she wouldn't look at him; certainly didn't want him to touch her - she was shutting him out and he didn't know why.

Fiona stood looking at her blue landscape. She'd had every intention of turning her hand to true life drawing, but her natural instinct to see everything from a long distance overcame her and without meaning to, she had reverted to being a landscape artist. Still, she was quite pleased with the result. Those beautiful curves and long sweeping lines were irresistible. She turned her canvas 180 degrees so the prone body became the sky, and nodded to herself in satisfaction.

"Shall we get a coffee before we head off?" Martin's voice broke her reverie.

"Not for me, I'm done for the day. Don't let me stop you though ..." She knew he couldn't stay on his own, it was not just a case of transport, but Martin was incapable of being on his own. He needed women - to flirt with, to look after. How could he show the world what a caring and loving man he was if he was on his own? She knew he would follow her, never out of sight or out of earshot; clinging like a limpet, a sucker fish, their former symbiotic relationship had become injurious. Martin just didn't know it yet.

Caroline was watching the interplay between Martin and his wife. She didn't want to be judgmental, but she thought his wife treated him really badly. He was so attentive and helpful but no matter what he did, his wife remained cold and dismissive. At next week's class she would be friendlier towards him - make an effort. They seemed an unlikely couple anyway, she with her punk hair and bohemian style, he in a suit. But Caroline knew more than most that outward appearances are not always what they seem.

CHAPTER 4 - JESSICA

NEVER ENOUGH

Having artists look at her as a thing of beauty, admiring her curves instead of being repulsed by them, seeing her as a normal person, not a greedy fat couch potato was a new experience for Jessica.

Weight had always been an issue for Jessica - it wasn't that she was lazy, in fact she had an enormous need to be on the move at every moment, her leg jigging up and down like a tic, playing Sudoku whilst watching television, reading a magazine whilst in the bath - not to do at least two things at once seemed an awful waste of time. No, she was active but there was always the feeling of never having enough; enough food, enough time, enough love. At Sunday lunch, her mum would bring round the roast potatoes "have as many as you want" she would say, but Jessica would count what was in the bowl and know that if she had as many as she wanted, she would have them all. There were never enough for her to have what she wanted so she would end her Sunday lunch still feeling hungry for something more. She hid food in her bedroom just in case; processed cheese triangles, cheese crackers, tinned ham. Nothing fresh that could go bad, but knowing it was there if needed kept her calm, and took the fear of hunger away. She had never actually been truly hungry but she feared it nonetheless. The panic of emptiness in the pit of her stomach, how it made her anxious and irritable, like an alcoholic she needed food NOW, any food, fast food, junk food, it didn't matter as long as it was immediate. Couldn't endure waiting for something to be cooked, couldn't wait to have her order taken in a restaurant, abject panic, what would happen to her if she couldn't find food? Jessica was intelligent enough to know she would not starve, but she just didn't know if her desperation would make her lash out in anger. The thought of making a fool of herself in public, making such an exhibition, created more anxiety. So she would stay in her room - hiding from the world and from herself, eating her hidden treasure, trying to fill the empty hole but never feeling satisfied. There was never enough.

Her mother took her to the doctor at age thirteen. Jessica could look back now and see that it was probably done from concern for her health and for her self-image, but when the doctor agreed that she needed to lose weight and suggested a diet, Jessica just saw that as proof that she was unacceptable, and she believed it to be true. All through secondary school, when her friends were going to the disco and having boyfriends and losing their virginity, she was in the background, only truly part of the group when they were trying out the latest fad diet.

Malcolm used to say she was an underachiever; wouldn't finish anything, but now she was proving him wrong and that made her triumphs at the art class even sweeter. Not that Malcolm would even know - he was part of her past now.

Malcolm was her first boyfriend - a setup date. Her first kiss. They were both virgins so when they eventually slept together, it was fine, but not the earth moving experience she was expecting. They would spend Sunday afternoons in his attic bedroom, listening to Led Zeppelin and having acceptable sex. Her mother took her to the doctor at age 18 to go on the pill. She went with Malcolm on a camping holiday to Newquay. He bought her flowers and sent her a letter in the post with just the three words 'I love you' on it. Jessica was so happy, relieved and grateful and of course she loved him too.

He proposed in Earl's Court car park at a Led Zeppelin concert. She lost lots of weight so she could get into her wedding dress and they were married in a church complete with white Rolls Royce, a marquee in the garden, sausage rolls and fairy cakes.

Malcolm didn't like it if she ate in public. It was OK to go out for a meal, but if they went to a party, she would go to the food table to get him a plateful but not have anything herself. Malcolm didn't like it if she wore jeans or trousers, even in the house. Malcolm didn't speak to her for three days because she had answered the front door without putting on her makeup. Jessica thought this must be normal, didn't know any better. Jessica was, after all, unacceptable. But Jessica also knew that she was losing weight, and soon she could be acceptable. She so wanted to be acceptable, to be like others. More than that she wanted to be approved of.

Lost as she was in thoughts from her past, she nearly missed her stop and had to quickly press the red bell before the driver pulled away again.

HOLIDAY PARK

Jessica lived with her parents in a static caravan park in Horton Regis on the South Coast of England. It wasn't how she had expected her life to turn out, still living with her parents at the age of 26, but after her divorce, and having nowhere else to go, it was the most practical thing. Anyway, her parents spent much of the year travelling; promoting their self-help fitness books, giving talks and attending sporting events. In effect, Jessica lived on her own in the caravan park.

She had not always lived here. Her family had lived close to the station of Ashbury Halt, the trains used to glide sedately past the bottom of their garden before stopping at the little station. Since the growing demand for speed and volume in the commuter belt, most trains shot straight through like a bullet. In the fullness of time, the old fashioned manual crossing gates were replaced with automated barriers as if a giant unseen hand was directing the flow of traffic. The once pretty little station, now unmanned and empty, crouched like a soulless grey sentry allowing trains to flash past but not stop. Ultimately the town, devoid of its lifeblood of incomers perished and died, becoming an unkempt backwater with little commerce, populated almost entirely by employees of the nuclear power plant a few miles outside town. Even the little Primary School had closed down and the kids bussed out each morning, like inmates of a prison shipped out daily to work on the chain gang.

Jessica was an only child. Her parents had long given up on the idea of having children and had sculpted their life accordingly. They were happy and fulfilled with just the two of them. When her mother found out she was pregnant, both parents were already in their forties and although they fleetingly considered abortion it wasn't really in their character, so they embraced this new project with enthusiasm. It all seemed such a splendid idea; it even sparked another self-help book *'How to be Forty, Fit and Fertile'*, but when Jessica was born and reality was forced upon them, they found this new lifestyle didn't suit them at all. They'd had 15 years of marriage before becoming pregnant. Fifteen years of being a solid loving couple with matching dreams and ambitions, only having to consider themselves when making decisions and now someone else had been added to the mix. It wasn't that they didn't love Jessica, it was more that she was superfluous to their lives. As time went on her parents slipped back into their comfortable self-absorbed routine, and Jessica slipped out of their minds.

When she was 14, Jessica's parents both took early retirement, sold up, and moved to the holiday park in Horton Regis. Although their static home was very compact, with all the park facilities at hand it felt like living in a 100 acre garden. Her parents hadn't considered how being uprooted would affect Jessica; leaving her friends, starting a new school in the middle of term in the midst of exams. She had never felt so lonely. In the summer the place was buzzing with holidaymakers; families and friends having fun. Another reminder that she didn't have that kind of family or any kind of friends. Jessica spent more and more time hiding away in their home eating; food was her friend and comfort.

As she grew older, her life revolved around the seasons of the holiday park. Summer meant lots of jobs around and money to be made. In the winter, there was little work and subsequently little income to go to the big city and party, even if she had the nerve or the friends to go with!

The holiday park became a sleepy reminder of Ashbury Halt peopled solely by the small community of residents who knew each other too well, and from whom you could not hide the indiscretions and embarrassments of the summer season. She had thought it would be an excellent place to find romance, but all she found in the summer were brief intense flings followed by long periods of despair when her holiday lover failed to keep up a long distance relationship. Each year became a seesaw of extremes. Short intense summers filled with high expectations and emotional disappointments and long dark winters with Saturday night pub quizzes and whist sessions. It was no surprise that Jessica felt she was unacceptable. The modelling job at the community centre was more than a means of making money in the off season, it had become a reason to feel validated and appreciated. Her very appearance had changed. She walked with her head held high. Looked people in the eye, smiled and people smiled back!

CHAPTER 5 - CAROLINE

HER NEWS

It was the morning before art class. Caroline was waiting excitedly in a coffee shop in the high street. This was one of her favourite places - in the summer she would sit outside at one of the patio tables on the pavement watching the world go by, and in the winter sit on one of the huge couches by the roaring log fire.

"Morning hun, thanks so much for coming, I didn't know who else to call?" Caroline got up from the table to greet her best friend.

Lou dumped her bags on the chair beside her, leaned across to hug Caroline and whispered.

"What's so important you couldn't tell me on the phone?"

"Oh Lou, I'm sorry, I didn't mean to scare you. It's all good" said Caroline grinning. "Take a look at this whilst I get the coffees. Cappuccino?"

Lou nodded and took the small flimsy piece of paper with what looked like a grainy black and white photo on it.

Caroline went up to the counter and ordered two cappuccinos. She was digging in her handbag for her loyalty card and looking back to see how Lou was reacting. When she returned with the coffees, Lou was still holding the paper and looking confused.

"Tah Dah! Surprise! What do you think?" said Caroline as if she had just produced a rabbit out of a hat.

"What is it? I mean I know WHAT it is, but who is it?"

"It's me! It's mine!" This wasn't quite the reaction Caroline was expecting "What's wrong?"

Lou seemed to relax a little, as if a balloon was slowly deflating inside her.

"Phew! I thought it might be JoAnn's"

"My daughter is only 15! I'm pretty sure I wouldn't be smiling if that was the case!"

"But you ARE smiling - are you happy about this?"

"Of course! Why wouldn't I be?"

"Oh I don't know, maybe because you already have two grown up girls! And you are 42! Does Mark know? Do the girls?"

"Mark knows, yes. Family night tonight, we are going to tell the girls then."

Lou dropped her voice and whispered "Is it his?"

"Of course it's bloody his! What a thing to say! You know better than anyone I wouldn't cheat on my husband!" Caroline regretted the words as soon as they were out of her mouth. "Sorry, Cheap shot."

"That's OK" said Lou flatly "It's not as if it's not true. We both know I've made mistakes in the past."

Caroline and Lou had been best friends since school and Caroline had always been the 'go to' person for Lou when relationships went wrong.

Caroline reached across the table and rested her hand on Lou's arm.

"I really am sorry." She whispered.

Lou looked up and saw the sincerity in her friend's eyes. She shook her head as if to clear it of thoughts. The effect was like Ctrl/Alt/Del - an emotional reboot bringing the conversation back to a point where their friendship was last solid.

"But how did it happen?"

Caroline raised an eyebrow and Lou burst out laughing, dispelling all remaining tension between the friends.

"I mean I know HOW it happened, but HOW did it happen?"

For the first time, Caroline looked sheepish as if she was being asked to voice a guilty secret. The word came out as a whisper - a sordid admission, a confession.

"Tequila."

CAROLINE

Caroline wasn't happy at all about her charcoal smudges from the first art class. She had disagreed with Patrick's methodology; all that rubbish about growing the picture. Whichever way you looked at it, it still resembled a scan of a foetus.

She missed her oil paints. She always saw her life as a whole palette of bright sunny colours, but there just wasn't time to do much painting in such a short session. The second class had been a bit better, but still she missed her colours. *Next week I shall use pencil rather than charcoal then I might develop my picture at home during the week* she thought.

But in truth, she wasn't happy with the result of the art class because she had been so diverted with real life. Here she was at 42, unexpectedly but blissfully pregnant. How many women would be horrified to be in her shoes? With JoAnn almost 15 and Beth already in year 7 she knew people would not understand her need to start a family again. As her daughters had grown older, they were becoming more independent - they no longer needed her to make princess costumes and run them to Brownies, Guides and netball matches. Caroline was immensely proud of her children and of herself for how she had brought them up, but right now she was suffering a bit of an identity crisis. If she was not a mother, what was her purpose?

That was why she joined the art class in the first place. She didn't need to work, in fact when she married, Mark had said he wanted an old-fashioned wife who looked after the home and children and allowed him to provide for them all. Caroline was happy with this, in fact it was quite a relief. Being a mother was the only role she felt she was any good at. Now that the children had grown up, learning to draw and paint was a perfect distraction – just like in a Jane Austen novel, it was an acceptable accomplishment for the wife of a gentleman. Maybe she would take up piano lessons next? Or maybe she would be back having no time for such luxuries when once again embroiled in nappies and spit-up. Well that would be just fine. For now, all she could feel was the warm glow of knowing a life was growing within her - a precious gift - a son. Privately she had always wanted a son, she wanted the kind of relationship that her daughters had with Mark - Mothers and sons, fathers and daughters - it had always been so.

She was sure her daughters would be okay with the idea, and Mark was thrilled, but there was always this cloud regarding Steven - with a new boy in the family, she wasn't sure how much longer she could keep quiet about Steven.

FAMILY NIGHT

Thursday night was family games night in the Armstrong house. Albeit rather an American custom that Caroline had discovered in her years spent across the pond, she had successfully made it her own, and Thursday night was sacrosanct.

When the girls were young it had been Monopoly, Snap and Cheat. Then, with the new Wii, it had been bowling and horse racing. The funniest times were doing the Penguin Shuffle – the screen showed a penguin on an ice flow and the aim was to stay on the ice by leaning one way or another on the balance board. The combination of seeing dad desperately leaning left and right, and the cartoon penguin shuffling all over the place was hysterical. Dad hopping on one leg to keep his balance as a penguin toppled into the water with a huge splash would have the whole room rolling about in fits of laughter.

But those days were gone, and the girls could only be persuaded to stay home for a blockbuster DVD and microwave popcorn. Caroline stopped by the video store to pick up this week's choice and the promised popcorn, which she put in her bag along with her scan and an email from Steven.

"What have you girls got for us tonight, then?" asked Mark as he came into the kitchen, loosening his tie and flopping down at the kitchen table.

"Twilight on the screen, and tacos on the table." Said Caroline as she placed a glass of red wine in his hand and a kiss on his head.

"It's quite a long movie Mum, can we eat in front of the telly tonight?"

"No Beth, tacos are really messy and salsa and sour cream dropped all over our carpet is not my idea of a good time. Anyway, Dad and I need to talk to you both, so we'll eat in here first."

Beth looked quizzically at JoAnn, who just shrugged. JoAnn was in the middle of an exhaustive texting session with a friend about whether or not their year 11 tutor was having an affair with the head of year 8. According to Amanda, Mr Carter had been seen whispering in Miss Peterson's ear whilst clearly snatching a grab at her arse, and apparently Miss Peterson didn't mind in the least. Amanda felt that Miss Peterson's silly smile and blushing cheeks served as proof positive that Mr Carter's hand was more than welcome wherever he was copping a feel. JoAnn thought this was much more interesting than anything Mum and Dad could say.

Caroline was really nervous about telling the girls her news. She had taken the email from Steven from her bag and had it in her pocket, along with the scan.

CHAPTER 6 - AUTUMN TERM

JUST ANOTHER THURSDAY

Jessica had caught an earlier bus so she could spend a little time in Horton Regis High Street. It reminded her of the High Street in Ashbury Halt but bigger and grander. She used to walk there on a Saturday, pocket money in hand looking in each shop window, working out what she could buy with what she had. It wasn't that she needed anything, it was the freedom of knowing she had the power to walk into a shop, any shop, and walk out with anything as long as it cost less than one week's pocket money. She liked the wool shop; all those different colours and textures, great fluffy balls of baby blue and sugar pink. She liked the cobbler; the smell of polish and leather wafting through the door, the magical key cutting machine and row upon row of blank keys of gold and silver; colours capturing the light like treasure.

She liked the model shop as well; mini replicas of steam trains and sports cars, Airfix kits and miniature tins of paint. There was a complete train setup in the window made to look like the real Ashbury Halt with miniature figures on the platform. She used to imagine the family group in the window was her standing between her mum and dad, holding their hands, everybody smiling.

She had a recurring dream that her parents had bought her from this shop for a pound. She dreamed that she was standing in the window on display, and they would point at her, haggle a bit with the shopkeeper, eventually hand over the pound and take her home. She had no idea why this dream, or nightmare, kept coming back to her, but as she got older she decided it was just her brain's way of explaining why she was so unlike her parents.

Horton Regis High Street was full of coffee shops, cafes and chemists. Her reminiscences of Ashbury Halt had left her feeling out of place, so she turned on her heels and marched determinedly to the Community Centre. She knew she was early but she was happy to sit in the studio and wait. She still didn't quite belong in the Community Centre in general, but she felt at home in the art studio; her special domain. When she got there the room was empty. Jessica sat quietly in the corner peacefully watching dust motes floating in the light streaming down from above, looking like tiny snowflakes in the sunshine.

Her peace was shattered as Martin burst through the double doors laden with artist paraphernalia and enthusing to his wife about the wonders of a beautiful day. She in turn followed him passively into the studio, ignoring both him and his performance. Jessica always thought theirs was a strange kind of marriage.

"See how wonderful the light is here? Even on a grey wintery day! ... Wonderful ... where do you want to set up Honey? ... OK, this looks good ... I'll get the water ..."

All the time Martin was chatting away, Fiona showed no reaction. Like a teenager with headphones existing in a world apart, going through the motions of setting up her workspace, zoning out her husband with his fussing and fretting.

"Right then, is there anything else you need? Anything I can do for you? No? OK, well I will be down in the coffee shop if you need me."

Martin waited expectantly for a few more seconds then turned on his heels and headed for the door. It closed quietly behind him, like a sigh, as if the room itself were exhaling and expelling all the tension.

"Morning."

Fiona looked up startled. She hadn't noticed Jessica sitting quietly in the corner. The effort of blocking out her husband meant she blocked out everything. Her face broke into a smile. She genuinely liked Jessica. She was an excellent model; always ready on time, conscious of the artist's needs, keeping still and choosing good poses both for aesthetics and for challenge.

"Hi Jessica" she said "lovely morning, albeit a bit chilly. Do you want the fan heater on today?"

The doors opened and the rest of the class came streaming through as one, shattering the oasis of peace with general chatter and the scraping of easels across lino as each artist set up their positions around the central space.

Over the previous couple of months Jessica had become much more relaxed in the class. Apart from that first time with Nick when he had wrapped her naked body in coils of rope. The students had been instructed to draw the coils of rope as if there was no body there at all - apparently it was an exercise in focussing on what you could see instead of what you thought you could see. The whole being tied up scenario was just as weird as the foetal blob episode with Patrick, but at least this time there were conspiring grins and chuckles from many of the women. Surprisingly it was also an exercise in becoming more relaxed in the class; it is hard to remain strangers when you are trussed up like the Sunday roast with everybody watching!

BODY LANGUAGE

Jessica thought back to the last life-class session, when she had realised what a unique position she was in. To all intents and purposes the whole class was studying her form. In fact, she spent the whole session looking at them.

Lost in their own worlds, they didn't realise that Jessica was watching them, studying them, analysing their body language and learning more about the artists as individuals than could ever be gleaned by social chit chat in the coffee break.

Take Martin for example. He originally came just as a helper for his wife – always there to lend support or assistance, getting water for paint or coffee and cake, but the last few sessions he had brought paper and charcoal, set up his own easel and was giving it a go.

From her viewpoint Jessica could see that it was all an elaborate act. Martin spent ages positioning his easel making it look like he was just trying for the optimum angle, when really he was edging closer and closer to Anthea – like a panther stalking a gazelle. Every so often he would lean over and praise her use of light and shade, or how she had captured the foot so well in that odd angle. It was obvious he felt safe and free from prying eyes, but then he didn't realize the inanimate object he was drawing had eyes and ears and senses. Jessica could also see that Fiona was watching him out of the corner of her eye. It was harder to interpret her body language though. Perhaps it was expected that she would be angry or hurt or ashamed, but her expression was almost whimsical.

Fiona watched Martin posturing and fawning over Anthea. She was a pretty girl and her beautiful black skin was taut and young and flawless. Martin seemed to be taking any and every opportunity to touch her – a gentle brush against her arm as she reached for more charcoal, a hand in the small of her back as he leaned over to admire her work, an arm around her shoulder as they stepped back to survey the finished piece.

Once upon a time Fiona would have felt hot knives stabbing at her belly; hot tears pricking her eyelids and the gut wrenching feeling of being totally alone. But not now. He thought he was invisible. He didn't realise how pathetic he looked to his wife. Pathetic, old, and overgrown. The light from the window that once would have highlighted his great bone structure and clear skin

47

now only emphasised the hairs in his ears and the same clear skin showing the thinning patch on his head. He may think of himself as a mighty cat ready to pounce on his prey, but really he was just the hyena, a rather grotesque scavenger grateful for anyone's left overs.

FIONA

Today was a good day for Fiona. She wasn't feeling sick at all and her hair had started to grow back in a funny spiky Annie Lennox way that suited her and made her feel younger and full of possibilities.

Before the cancer all her artistic creativity had been channelled into landscapes. The home she shared with her husband sat on the cliffs at Horton Regis and allowed stunning views over the Solent, the Isle of Wight and the English Channel. All the changing colours and moods of the sea and sky combined with the seasonal changes; from bare windswept branches to hedgerows laden with late summer blackberries. It was the perfect location for a watercolourist.

Since her illness however, her sights were attracted to Life Drawing. Perhaps it was the wonders of the human body and how it can endure and cure itself? She couldn't be absolutely sure that she was cured of course – that would take time and future appointments with the Oncologist to make sure she was all still clear, but in the meantime she had every intention of living life to the full.

Joining the studio had been a great opportunity to try something new and a chance to meet like-minded people. Martin had insisted on accompanying her, avowing himself a dutiful and concerned husband. He was so charming, even with his silvering hair he had not lost all his good looks and his gentlemanly manner. He had been both beautiful and rugged, and she had been desperately in love with him for many years. If she had been less in love she might have left him over his philandering, but in the early years of their marriage a life without Martin seemed as pointless as it did painful.

After every affair ended he would come charmingly back to their marital bed, full of love and promises. Fiona would take him back with a warm embrace, but soon enough he would start to turn away from her advances and she would know another woman was keeping him warm whilst she stayed out in the cold. As the years and the affairs rolled by Fiona became hardened towards him. The times when his heart and body were elsewhere, she built an independent life for herself with friends and hobbies and above all painting. Only now, when there was a risk of losing her entirely had Martin promised himself devotedly to her. It was all too little too late. Fiona found herself irritated beyond measure at his sycophantic behaviour. The more he advanced, the further she retreated. Now here he was accompanying her to the art class; helping carry her easel and materials, getting her coffee at the break, being charming to everyone. This invasion of her independence and her privacy was threatening to take the pleasure out of her new-found hobby – her fellow students would look at her as the bitch in the relationship and shower sympathy on the husband. The hypocrisy of it was almost too much to bear.

But bear it she would. Having her health back was proving rather a contradictory state of affairs. Of course, there is nothing like the threat of impending death to give oneself a kick up the backside, to appreciate the absolute importance of life at any cost, but it also made her painfully aware of a life wasted.

Fiona found she was cross with herself, more so than being cross with Martin. She saw life now as such a precious gift. The fact that she had squandered so many years on such an undeserving recipient as her husband embarrassed her.

Well no more. She had made a hard decision. It didn't matter whether Martin noticed or not; she didn't need revenge or validation, but the fact was, her life - however much she had left of it, was going to be hers and hers alone.

CHAPTER 7 - AUTUMN TERM 2

CARIBBEAN COOKING

"Morning everyone. Hi Anthea, did you see that cooking programme yesterday about the Caribbean?"

"No – what was it on?"

"ITV or something. I'm sure you can get it on iPlayer."

"Why – what's it about?"

"Oh, local cuisine, local cooking methods, things like that. They have these huge oil drums that were converted to great big barbecue grills – you could fit a whole pig on one!"

"I'll check it out when I get home. Did it still have its head on?"

"What? No! There wasn't actually a whole pig, it was just big enough to fit one. You are just too literal!"

"Literally busting actually." Said Anthea bobbing about on the spot. "Back in a mo. – don't start without me."

"Did you see it. Caroline?" Jessica asked.

"See what?"

"The programme about cooking in the Caribbean? Didn't you say your son was there?

"Oh right. Yes. No. I mean - no I didn't see the programme but yes, Steven is in Antigua. Running a yacht."

"That must be lovely. They showed Antigua and all the cruise ships and sailboats, the water is an incredible blue and it all looks so lush and – well, tropical."

"I wouldn't know, I've never been."

"You haven't been to the Caribbean? To see your son?"

"I've been to Tobago".

"What was that like?"

"Hot. Beautiful beaches but hot. I was actually glad to get back home. To be honest, England in the spring and summer cannot be beaten"

"Oh well, maybe Anthea can bring back pictures for you - what did you say the boat was called?"

"Oh I don't remember" snapped Caroline, "I can't be expected to know the name of everything."

Jessica was often nonplussed by Caroline. She was positively mercurial – warm and gushing one minute and a complete cold fish the next. Jessica left Caroline re-sorting her paints into straight lines, and headed to the couch to take up her position.

COFFEE TIME AGAIN

After so many weeks together the art class had become quite a tight knit group, the coffee break was now full of friendly chat and gossip. Jessica had even started joining the group, padding barefoot through the corridors wearing only her robe. Anthea had given her the courage to join them all in the coffee shop, assuring her that everyone there was a friend, and anyone else would just think she was gutsy and brave. There were lots of times lately that Jessica felt her life had improved because of Anthea; the first true friend she had ever had.

Today, following the conversation in the studio about Caribbean cooking Martin squeezed a chair next to Anthea and was asking her about Antigua,

"Did you like it there? Do you miss it?" he asked, oozing charm. His body language was so obvious; half turned in his chair to face Anthea, leaning towards her, elbow on the table to rest his temple on, creating a scene of privacy. Fiona watched him from across the table. He was really good at the charm offensive, but totally unaware of his recipient's body language. He didn't seem to notice that Anthea had edged away; moving her coffee cup and half eaten banana, making her own private space to exclude Martin. Fiona smiled and let out a soft chuckle at the idiocy of her husband.

"Antigua? Well no, I've never been to the Caribbean. My father came from there but I was born in England. I'm going out at Christmas for the first time though." Anthea's stumbled response was aimed at the table at large to escape the cloying attentions of Martin.

"How wonderful!" said Fiona, throwing her a lifeline so she could turn away from Martin, "you might even meet up with Caroline's son!"

"What? What was that?" Caroline had been on the phone and hadn't followed the conversation and Fiona said again that when Anthea went to Antigua she could meet up with Steven and wouldn't that be nice for Caroline?

There was a long pause. Everyone was looking at Caroline for a response; a smile, or enthusiasm. Instead, Caroline looked like a deer caught in the headlights. There was an awkwardness as the group sat in confused silence until Liz, a rather priggish pretentious class member sitting at the end of the table, grabbed the crumbs of conversation, and steam rolled ahead with her own anecdotes.

"Oh, how wonderful! I was in Antigua last year – you will love it – great shopping opportunities, my husband bought me an emerald ring. Of course the beach is fabulous, although you do need to be vigilant with people walking along the beach trying to sell you things; the most ridiculous homemade bracelets and tacky tee shirts and stuff."

"You sound as if you got to know it quite well." said Fiona "How long were you there?"

"Oh, just a day, we were on a cruise through the islands and stopped at a different port every night. But the islands are not big, Antigua is the same size as our very own Isle of Wight, so really small!

"Of course we could have chosen to do a number of things. Some friends went on an island tour, but sitting for an hour or more driving around in an air-conditioned minibus didn't really appeal. We prefer to absorb the atmosphere and get in with the natives. For lunch we went local and found this adorable little place in a side street of St. John's- that's the capital. Richard had pasta vongole which had locally caught Antiguan clams. He said it was delicious but I'm a little wary of locally gathered shellfish. You don't know how clean it is do you? I played safe and had lasagne, but it was very passable."

Liz might have hoped for some appreciation of her tales of adventure on a day trip to Antigua, but as she had hardly taken time to draw breath in the telling of it, the coffee break had ended and those at the table started to leave.

"Well that was painful." whispered Anthea as Jessica shoved in the last bite of cake and they got up to leave. "I swear, if I said I had an elephant, she would have a box to put it in!" Jessica snorted and nearly spat out the remains of her brownie.

ANTHEA ANGRY

The awkwardness of the coffee break was still there during the second half of the class. Some kind of unspoken friction lay between Caroline and Anthea. After the class ended and Jessica was getting dressed, she got a text alert. She had got as far as her underwear but couldn't find her glasses to read the text. It was gloomy behind her screen so she waited for everyone to clear the studio before stepping out into the light and rummaging in her bag to get her glasses. The text was from Anthea 'OMG meet in loo in 10' Jessica continued getting dressed, then headed for the ladies.

Anthea was leaning across the hand basin, hands clenched tightly as if she was afraid she would not be able to hold on, eyes screwed up in fury. She looked like she was either about to explode or to burst into wracking sobs.

"What's the matter? Are you OK?" Anthea jumped back surprised at the voice behind her, unaware that Jessica was there.

"No I am not bloody OK! I hate that racist bitch!"

"Who?"

"Miss bloody perfect! Caroline sodding Armstrong!"

"What on earth has she done? And why racist? She never came across that way to me?"

"Course not! You're the wrong bloody colour!"

Anthea started to tell Jessica about how she had lived with racial prejudice all her life. She had been born in London to an English mother but her absentee father was West Indian and all her life people asked her where she was from.

"Does anyone ask you where you are from? No! Because you're white!"

Jessica was a bit flummoxed by that and struggled for a suitable response.

"Maybe they are just interested?" she said.

"What – that I come from Fulham? Does that somehow make me exotic?!"

"I don't know. Sorry. It must be hard…"

"Yeah – well – sorry to go off on one, but Miss Perfect up there just rubbed me up the wrong way"

"What happened?"

"She just cornered me in the corridor. I thought she wanted to explain about her odd behaviour at coffee break. Then she was overflowing with comments saying how I would probably not move in the same social circles; how Steven was really busy and probably out on charter, and it's really busy in the season etc etc. She was so negative, like she really doesn't want me to meet up with her son."

Jessica remained quiet, giving Anthea time to settle.

"The thing is," Anthea continued, "it's quite likely that I *will* bump into Steven – it's not like trying to meet up with someone in New York – the whole bloody island is no bigger than the Isle of Wight for God's sake!"

"I don't know what to say. Maybe it was just miscommunication?"

"I really don't think so. She even had the nerve to say he probably didn't mix with many locals, meaning blacks presumably and that the yachting industry are mainly ex-pats which I think means rich and white." Anthea wasn't shouting now, she was almost whispering as if the words were hard to get out; as if she was embarrassed to voice this admission that she was neither a local or a rich ex-pat, and that Caroline was probably right and they wouldn't mix in the same circles.

Jessica was a bit concerned about Anthea's outburst. She had always viewed Caroline as a very self-controlled, polite and conscientious person. She just didn't seem the racist type. Then again she hadn't been dealing with racism her whole life like Anthea had. She hated to see her friend so miserable.

"You know what this calls for?" said Jessica taking control of the situation and picking up their bags, "TEA"

"Tea!" said Anthea in a horrified voice.

"Long Island Iced Tea!" said Jessica with a smile "and lots of it!" and they both laughed and headed out towards the High Street.

RACIST?

Caroline felt guilty and worried in equal measure as she drove home from class. She really was not the slightest bit racist and had not intended to hurt Anthea's feelings, but she really *really* didn't want her poking her nose around Antigua and finding out the truth about Steven...

Her husband had known about Steven even before they were married. After one drunken summer barbecue when they were lying together on the grass, all warm and glassy eyed due in part from a few puffs of a spliff they had shared, Mark talked about his family, about his sister-in-law who was desperate for children but couldn't have any, about his own yearning for masses of kids.

In the security of their secret bubble, stars above and warm grass below, Caroline told him about living in America and getting pregnant and how wonderful it felt. She told him how she had left the father and son in America; how hard it had been.

She knew that her secret admission about having children was a huge factor in Mark proposing to her. The summer barbecue represented a magical moment in her life. She had shared a secret from her past, yet Mark had accepted her and she knew she would never feel alone again.

But the cloud was rising once more. Mark thought he knew the truth, but Caroline knew it was only part of the truth, that the lie had grown over the years and spread beyond control. Now her children would ask after Steven, would be interested in his photos and emails; but it was all a lie. The lie had built and swelled until even Caroline herself believed in it to some degree.

Now she was pregnant again. Knowing this, and knowing it was a boy, made the lie poisonous. How could her family accept her when they knew.

CHAPTER 8 - CHRISTMAS

LAST DAY XMAS

The last day of term and the class was not in quite such a hurry to head off into the cold weather. The light and camaraderie within the studio compared with the icy rain and dark shadows outside kept everyone back a little longer. Martin suggested they should celebrate the holiday season with a festive drink in the pub up the road. Although a few of the group made excuses and slid off to do their last minute shopping, the majority of the class rushed out to their cars to deposit all the paraphernalia associated with the art class and regrouped at a table in the window of the Red Lion.

Unlike their usual foray into the coffee shop with its genteel atmosphere, the pub was alive with laughter and snippets of disjointed conversation. The rain and wind outside brought people together as they sought warmth and companionship around the logs burning in the grate. Fairy lights and candles cast an orange glow off the old walls and horse brasses; the smell of mulled wine and wood smoke lay over the gathering.

Caroline was trying to hand out invitations to her After Christmas Drinks Party, but only surreptitiously to people she really wanted to attend. Fiona didn't expect to receive one, but Martin was already gushing to Caroline about how they would be *delighted to come.* Anthea would be on holiday in the Caribbean so

Caroline didn't worry about the need to invite her, but Jessica was invited, as was Nick.

Jessica sat quietly between the artists, not really sure of her place. She felt weirdly vulnerable socialising amongst the group whilst being fully clothed, knowing they could be imagining her naked, especially Martin - it was something she had not experienced outside the bounds of the Community Centre before. It was difficult to know if she was part of the group, part of the class, or whether the class viewed her as staff.

Christmas had never been much of a favourite time for Jessica - she looked awful in sparkly red dresses and she didn't have the sort of income that would allow her to buy all the gifts she wanted to give, but every year she made the effort to slog over to Southampton on the train to shop. This time however, she had her modelling fees to spend. Despite the weather outside, things didn't seem as grey today as she tucked the invite in her bag, picked up her stuff, wished everyone a merry Christmas and headed out into the winter rain with a smile on her face.

NICK CHRISTMAS

Nick's invite to Caroline's party included a +1. He was pretty sure this was an investigative ploy to see if he brought a date - and whether the date would be female. He smiled secretly at the undisguised tactic, but actually he wasn't sure there was anyone he wanted to have as his date at all.

Nick knew people thought he was gay, and would be surprised to hear he was very much heterosexual. Or at least had been. The problem was that things didn't really work 'down there' anymore. As with many other areas of his life, it was something he didn't talk about or want people to know. He didn't have a mass of male friends other than his Army mates. Gay men sensed he was straight so largely ignored him, straight men though he was gay and excluded him from such manly pursuits as rugby matches and weight training; they didn't want to risk being caught out with him in the showers when the soap dropped. Women, however, found him irresistible; handsome, rugged, and being gay, slightly vulnerable but totally safe. Unfortunately, none of these scenarios added up to a friend.

Christmas was never a great time for Nick. It was just another reminder of his wife leaving him. They had met at a life drawing class; Jenny was the model, Nick the art student. Nick was strong both physically and emotionally. Jenny was beautiful and fragile; their sexual chemistry was extraordinary. It had been a match made in heaven with Nick the alpha male taking care of Jenny. They weren't divorced, and they both still loved each other, but things had changed since his time in the army; it all got complicated.

When he was on tour in Afghanistan, he had worried so much about Jenny running off with Rifleman Archer. Stupid in retrospect; there had never been any reason to distrust Jenny, but worry added to fear, added to stress and periods of severe stress are always bad for your health.

Looking back to that night in Afghanistan when he literally dodged a bullet, he knew now that the tingling he had felt in his hands was not from sleeping badly but was one of the symptoms of his first 'episode'. After many tests and hospital visits, he had been diagnosed with Remitting Relapsing Multiple Sclerosis. He was invalided out of the Army, given a war pension, and left to his own devices. There was no cure.

Jenny did not accept the role of carer willingly, any more than Nick acknowledging he needed help. It was emasculating to need help in the shower, he hated not being able to work. Jenny had to cut down her own working hours to care for him, and she missed her freedom. Both missed the security and camaraderie of military life. Although he could still provide for Jenny financially, he was incapable of getting an erection and had no sex drive at all. It was unfair on them both. Too much had changed; the important things that brought them together, the sexual chemistry, their plans and dreams, their roles in a marriage - the gaps had become too wide. When Jenny was offered a job in Oxford, they both agreed to part and live an open marriage. There were no arguments, no recriminations, no choices.

Nick had framed one of the drawings he had made of her and kept it in his bedroom.

He didn't tell anyone. There wasn't really anyone to tell.

JESSICA CHRISTMAS

Jessica had a terrible Christmas with her parents. They had come back from New Zealand where they had been giving a round of talks in Queenstown. Mum had been bungy jumping off Skipper's bridge and had sprained her wrist. Unable to cook Christmas dinner (or much else), it was left to Jessica to cook and clean and care for her parents. This gave them every opportunity to criticise and complain; she had cooked too much food, the wine was too cold, the decorations too over the top.

December 27th - Jessica's parents had arranged for a few of their friends to come round for drinks; a soiree as Mum called it. It was the day of Caroline's drinks party and although she had been invited, Jessica was weighing up the pros and cons to see if she wanted to go. Cons: she was friends with Anthea and didn't want to be seen as siding with Caroline, knowing how Anthea felt about her. Pros: if she stayed for this stupid family soiree she would be expected to be the hostess/waitress/washer-up.

After years of being told she was not good enough by her parents, her time as a life model had shown her that even if she was never going to be acceptable to them, she was definitely good enough for others. Jessica was starting to appreciate that her parents were completely self-absorbed; they didn't need her to complete their lives, they had each other. All her life she had tried to please them, to be loved by them, to be appreciated by them. All her life she had felt unacceptable. She was beginning to see things from another perspective; maybe her conception had been a mistake, maybe they never wanted children at all, maybe she had been invited to live with them after her divorce just so she could be caretaker of the static home. She always thought it was <u>her</u>, when actually it was <u>them</u>!

Jessica opened her closet, took out her new high heeled scarlet shoes, her soft scarlet Pashmina and phoned for a taxi.

Christmas Party

Mark was in the bedroom pulling a tie from the rack in the fitted wardrobe. As he slid the door closed, he caught sight of himself in the long mirror. For a second he was confused, not recognising his own reflection. He so rarely spent time considering himself that he was shocked by what he saw. Okay, so he was older, grey flecks in his hair, his face pale above a growing double chin, but it was the suit that said it all. A smartly dressed middle aged successful businessman: partner in Blatch and Woolpike Tax Accountants, treasurer for the Yacht Club, parent governor at his daughters' school. This image he saw, his outward presentment no longer matched the person inside. Had it ever really done so? Had he always been just a suit? He wasn't sure he could remember.

"Are you nearly ready Mark?" said Caroline as she huffed and puffed her way up the stairs. She entered their bedroom and made straight for the bed, one hand in the small of her back and the other under her bump. She managed to roll onto the bed and kick off her shoes, letting out a rush of air halfway between a sigh and a grunt. She watched Mark as he stood very still in front of the mirror.

"Is everything OK?" she asked.

"When did I just become a suit?" he said, still looking in the mirror.

"What do you mean?" Caroline rolled onto her back and closed her eyes.

Mark turned away from the mirror at last and looked with compassion at his wife. This pregnancy had really taken its toll on her. When she told him she was pregnant it had been wonderful, exciting and rejuvenating. They both felt younger than their years, keen to take on the challenge, sure of their abilities. This situation had not been planned but it was done and couldn't be undone. Getting rid of the baby, having an termination, was never an option. Mark was a staunch pro-lifer. He hated that the younger generations treated abortion as a form of birth control, and so they both embraced the situation determined to make it work, Team Armstrong.

He went over to the bed looking tenderly at Caroline. She looked exhausted. He gently lifted the hair that had fallen across her face, laying under her nose so that every out breath made it flutter. Mark bent down and kissed her softly on the forehead. She opened her eyes and looked at him.

"Team Armstrong kiddo" he said.

"Team Armstrong" she smiled.

It had always been their thing; whatever problems came their way, they knew they could cope with it as a team. Together they were strong. "Strong is already in our name!" he would say and she would be relieved knowing Mark always had her back.

"Let's go down together." said Mark, offering his arm for support.

Jessica was glad she had come. Caroline's after Christmas party was wonderful. The house was immaculate and very posh, the food and drink were fantastic, Christmas decorations all colour coordinated and very classy. Jessica also saw how the family treated each other; there was love and respect between parents and children that was really genuine. She thought how it must feel to be like Caroline and have everything she ever wanted.

Fiona was sitting with Nick and Caroline, and Jessica went to join them.

"Your house is absolutely beautiful Caroline." she said. She wanted to say that Caroline looked beautiful too, but in all honesty she looked terrible.

The four of them chatted pleasantly for a while until Caroline's daughter Beth came to top up glasses just as Jessica was telling them about Anthea's adventures in Antigua.

"Ooh, that's where our brother lives! He's on a yacht there." piped up Beth.

It was as if a window had been opened and cold air poured over the group. Caroline shivered as if a someone had walked over her grave.

Chapter 9 - Antigua

Anthea to Antigua

Anthea was really excited as the plane came into land at VC Bird International airport in Antigua. She had been looking out of the window as they descended, and couldn't help feeling that the view was almost surreal. Was the sea really that blue and the island so green?

As usual, as soon as the seatbelt sign was switched off the majority of passengers leapt up from their seats as if spring-loaded. Anthea was tucked away in a window seat and had to wait until the elderly couple next to her had moved off before she could collect her bag and coat from the overhead locker.

When she finally reached the doorway and made her way down the steps the heat hit her as if she had opened the oven door on a full Sunday roast. There were no buses to take them to the terminal, just a short walk across the hot tarmac. The sound of jet engines and smell of aviation fuel at odds with the palm trees all around. Anthea felt quite stupid carrying her coat in such heat, but it had been about 6° C in London when she left: it was way more than that in Antigua.

As they passed through the covered walkway at the entrance to the terminal passengers were offered local rum punch by young girls in bright orange checked costumes and entertained by Steel Band music over the

PA system. After eight hours cramped in a seat where it felt that everything one owned was balancing on a tiny tray table and liable to be knocked over with every squirm in an effort to find comfort, it all seemed a little contrived. She was very aware that the whole "welcome to Antigua" experience would be a greater memory in the retelling than it was in reality. The clocks might say it was only 2 PM but it felt like 10 o'clock at night. Many of her fellow passengers were looking pale and exhausted, just wanting to get to their respective swimming pools to start their holiday properly.

In the immigration hall a ground hostess was directing pedestrian traffic. There were already two long lines waiting to have their passports stamped, but Anthea was directed towards a much shorter queue. The sweat was already beginning to run down her back and she could see the luggage conveyor at the other end of the room disgorging all manner of bags and boxes. Anthea was concerned about losing her bag with all the gifts for her relatives so she had been inching forward in the queue. She had just spotted the pink ribbons on her suitcase as it disappeared off the end of the conveyor belt when a deep voice boomed

"Keep behind the yellow line until you are called!"

Anthea looked around and realise the shout was directed at her. She had not registered that she had reached the front of the line, and although there were no other passengers at the immigration desk, she dutifully stepped back one pace.

"Next" called the burly immigration officer and Anthea approached the desk feeling like this was a trip to the headmaster's office. She had filled in her immigration form on the plane and handed it to the officer together with her passport with a friendly smile.

The officer, however, did not smile back. She was heavyset and quite formidable with a complicated and elaborate hairdo of braids and corn rolls that seemed at odds with the starchily pressed uniform. She picked up the passport and form as if they were something unidentifiable and rather distasteful.

"Why are you coming through the Nationals line?"

"I was told to join this line by the lady at the entrance".

"Did you tell her you were an Antigua National?"

"No, I didn't say anything. She just pointed for me to come here". Anthea was feeling a bit miffed at how she was being treated and it obviously came across in her voice.

The officer pushed the immigration form and passport back to her, "well that's wrong. I can't deal with you here you will have to go back... Next!"

Anthea, having been summarily dismissed, picked up her bags again and joined the back of one of the long queues. Apart from the humiliation of people thinking she was a queue jumper she was incensed about wasting time and also the dawning realisation of what it had really all been about. It was all to do with the colour of her skin. The woman at the entrance had just looked at her and presumed, wrongly, that she was a local West

Indian. Her reception at the immigration desk was so unfriendly because the immigration officer probably thought she was trying to impersonate a West Indian. At the end of the day it was a clear message that she didn't belong here either. Just like in England people looked at the colour of her skin and decided that she was an alien - an interloper.

PROUD VILLAGE

Byron was already waiting outside when Anthea got through Customs. He held a sign in front of him with her name on it; they had sent pictures to each other over the years but is was comforting to know they didn't have to rely on recognition amongst a sea of strangers.

Byron had taught technical drawing at the High School in St. John's, but was retired from teaching and drove a taxi instead. Unlike England, where taxis were either black cabs or saloon cars, here almost every taxi was a minibus. Fares were set from point A to point B rather than how long the journey was as you couldn't really guess the time it might take. Traffic often came to a standstill if goats were in the road, or a cow sauntered across, or even because drivers just stopped to chat to a friend coming in the opposite direction. It took nearly an hour to drive the 18 miles to English Harbour. At first conversation was a bit awkward, but Byron was so excited to have his beautiful daughter here in Antigua, he had made lots of plans to show her around and show her off.

Anthea was staying in Proud Village where her father had rented a basic West Indian cottage within walking distance of the bars and marinas of English Harbour. There was nothing Proud about the house or the village. It was named after the Proud family who owned the eight acres of land where they had built twenty or so rental properties.

It was 4pm by the time Anthea got settled. Byron had left her to unpack and arrived back at 5 with a few basic groceries to see her through the night and a couple of cold beers to enjoy on the tiny decking outside the front door. All the houses on the plot were of similar design, built from breeze blocks and plywood or planking. All had corrugated steel roofs and small decking areas, and were dotted casually across the property with pathways between and communal spots with barbecue areas and seating. The accommodations were very modest, but there was activity everywhere and lots to look at.

Byron carried two plastic chairs onto the tiny balcony, and found a bucket under the sink which, when turned upside down made an acceptable table. He had brought a mosquito coil with him and set it up on a saucer showing Anthea how to light the end and blow it out so it was just smouldering, letting the smoke drift to keep the mosquitos away.

Anthea was incredibly tired; it had been a big day both physically and emotionally. She wanted to sleep but didn't want to miss anything. At first she was a bit nervous about staying in a house all on her own, but it was soon obvious that with all the houses close by and the general hubbub, she would not feel lonely.

Byron was not a great one for small talk and Anthea was too tired to string a sentence together, so they just sat quietly on the deck, their feet on the railings, sipping cold Carib beer and watching the world go by. It was after 10 when Anthea finally crawled into bed.

Anthea woke and looked at her watch - 5 a.m. - it felt like she hadn't slept at all. There had been noises everywhere: the chirping of what Anthea thought were cicadas but turned out to be tree frogs, music blaring through the open window of one of the other houses, some kind of live music from one of the bars in the harbour, mosquitos buzzing round her ears, shouts and laughter from a constant stream of people coming and going past her windows. As if all that was not enough, she could have sworn she heard a shotgun go off!

She was not really a morning person but even at this early hour the temperature was rising, and she felt the need to go outside. Anthea got up and padded barefoot to the kitchen area, filled the kettle and lit the gas stove. While the water heated she found the tea bags, sugar and long-life milk that Byron had brought her. When her tea was ready she unlocked the front door and sat out on the decking to enjoy her first morning.

The remains of the mosquito coil she had forgotten to extinguish had left a perfect coil of fallen ash on the saucer. Not a breath of wind had disturbed the ash in the night. She was just thinking what a clever idea the coil was when she realized her legs were covered in little red spots. Twenty six mosquito bites on one leg in one night. So much for the coil! Luckily her skin hadn't reacted and turned the bites into itchy welts. *A useful aspect of having Antiguan blood* she thought with a smile. She sat back admiring the swaying banana leaves, the clean air and the warm breeze on her skin. Paradise. She took a long gulp of tea and immediately spat it out - Disgusting!

ANTIGUA LIVING

Over the next few days Anthea learned a lot about her roots. She learned never to fill the kettle from the tap; a combination of high levels of chlorine mixed with rusted pipes and mud seeping into the water supply made tea undrinkable. She learned that only tourists walk on the sunny side of the road; locals stay cool in the shade. She learned there is no point going out in the rain and getting wet, much better to wait twenty minutes for the rain to stop. She learned that cows and goats and sheep had no respect for road traffic or garden flowers. She tried local food such as Chicken Roti and Goat Curry which she loved, as well as Saltfish and Fungi which she hated.

Anthea's father's family was extensive. There were Spencers all across the island; from Falmouth to Fitches Creek, Swetes, Old Road and everywhere in between. When Byron took her on a tour of the island, they had to stop in almost every village and meet cousins and aunties. When he took her to his home she met brothers and sisters too. After leaving Anthea's mother, Byron had returned to Antigua harbouring the belief that he was not cut out to be a father. It had not been long before Byron met his current wife, Kendra, and soon after that he became a father for the second time. Anthea thought it might be awkward meeting his wife and children, but they were genuinely pleased to see her. Kendra already had one daughter, Janella, by the time she met Byron at a church BBQ and they had two sons together. Everyone lived in a sprawling property on an acre of land in Buckleys in the middle of the island. Janella lived in her own cottage on the property with her three year old son. Anthea just loved how close the family was, how welcoming, and how they made her feel included.

Such a small island, yet two very different lifestyles: rainforest and beach, Antiguan and Expat, employed and tourist. Anthea thought there would be tension and prejudice but it just didn't seem to be the case; everyone co-existing in harmony. It was so comfortable. For the rest of the Christmas holidays Anthea spent half her time with her family in Buckleys and half in the bars and boats of English Harbour.

CHAPTER 10 - 1989 CARO

LOVE

There had never been a love like theirs. Romantic novels, Mr Darcy and Elizabeth Bennet, Heathcliff and Kathy, nothing came close to the reality of Caroline and Steve. They were as one - they thought the same, wanted the same things, dreamed and planned together, and talked. They never stopped communicating - talking about their day, their wishes and dreams and adventures to come. Their love was so large and all-encompassing there was just no room for anyone else to exist between them. They were one unit, one entity. They knew they would be together forever. He said he hoped he died before her. She said if he died she would kill herself rather than go to his funeral.

But Caroline knew statistics proved that husbands died before their wives, so every night she wouldn't fall asleep with her back to him - she would roll over and watch him, and smile, knowing that the last thing she saw each night before falling asleep was the love of her life.

Caro and Steve never married. It really wasn't necessary. One day they would marry, but it wouldn't make any difference. They were a couple, together in the truest sense - whether it was sanctioned in a church or before a judge was irrelevant.

They had met at the Ft Lauderdale Boat Show. Steve was a yacht captain - skipper of a luxury Swan 65 private charter sailboat, Caro a three year employee of a London travel agency on her first fact finding trip to consider the feasibility of breaking into the yacht charter holiday market.

In the days pre Aids but post 'the pill', free love was as widely practiced as in the '60s. The heady mix of youth, money and adventure, served with copious quantities of champagne and rum, made the Boat Show dock parties in Ft Lauderdale legendary.

Caro remembered the first time she set eyes on Steve - climbing off the boat with a bag full of empty bottles.

"Morning ma'am, you missed a good night last night." He said shaking his bag of glass empties.

"So it seems" Caro was rather embarrassed that she had been caught obviously judging the alcohol consumption, but at least he hadn't spotted her judging his strong thighs!

At yet another dock party that night, they had sought each other out, and in a really short space of time became inseparable - it was inevitable, meant to be.

Eight weeks after the last marquee and bar had been removed from the marinas, Steve and Caro moved into an apartment in Ft Lauderdale. Caro left her job in London, given notice on her flat, and been signed on as Steve's crew to circumvent any Visa issues she may have had being in USA. No-one was surprised at the speed of their relationship, it was obvious they were meant to be together.

Steve was only a little taller than Caro - when they embraced she fitted perfectly just below his nose. She felt again his soft full lips brush her forehead, like a blessing. At night she would curl up in the curve of his armpit, her cheek on the smoothness of his chest, and know that nothing in the world could harm her. Caro felt she had never made love before she met Steve. Not to say she had never had sex before, or indeed never had an orgasm, but with Steve it was so different. She was always ready for him, and he her. A look or a touch would make her breath catch, and like a switch being turned on she could feel every muscle in her core flutter and contract so that each outward breath shuddered. When they kissed, her legs and arms became weak - all heat and energy drawing inward and downward making an aching need that begged to be satisfied. A guttural groan the only escaping sound. If Steve had not been there to hold her, she would have simply melted into the ground.

As their bodies moved together in perfect rhythm and perfect fit, slowly and sensually each thrust bringing her closer to exquisite bliss, yet knowing that to reach the peak would bring an end to this sensual abandonment, wanting but not wanting, the tide rising and falling, stop! Don't stop!, an obsession, an addiction, cannot stop, don't want it to end, a cruel dichotomy.

The relief; total exhaustion of mind and body, every nerve ending and muscle sensitive to involuntary spasms, twitching and shuddering. A tear or two rolling down onto the pillow - an expression of something so profound shared and exquisite beauty ended.

SEASICK

Caro couldn't look at Steve without feeling a falling sensation in the pit of her stomach. She would die rather than lose him - do anything for him. They loved each other so much, nothing else mattered.

The trip down to the Caribbean was almost perfect. Just the two of them in a world of their own.

Sitting at the chart table, Caro pulled out the log book to mark their noon position. It was hard to imagine the days when a sextant and chronometer were essential pieces of kit. Steve could still take sun sights and find stars for navigation, but it was really just for practice, keeping his hand in should the Sat Nav fail.

Caro liked the responsibility of updating the log book. The padded cover and thick pages telling a story with just a few lines of comment.

Nov 17th - no wind again today. Big swell from storm 50N. 2100: saw the lights of Nassau.

Nov 20th - hove-to under reefed main.

Nov 23rd - Saw 8 dolphins play in the bow wave. 1730 made Road Town.

All the entries in her own tidy penmanship.

Caro carefully marked their position on the chart just as Steve had taught her, and returned the log book and pencils back in their racks so they couldn't fall out all over the place if it got rough.

She had only been down below for about ten minutes, but was already starting to feel seasick again. This was the only cloud on her horizon - if she couldn't overcome this hurdle she was never going to make it as charter crew.

Chapter 11 - January

Back to School Caroline

A new year and a new term. it was also going to be Caroline's last session - her pregnancy was so advanced that she found it hard to be creative in the art class; the smell of turpentine made her feel sick, the constant trips to the loo, struggling up the stairs with all her art supplies. It was time to call it a day.

Caroline felt huge. This pregnancy was much harder than the others. She didn't know if it was her age or because this time it was a boy. Morning sickness had been terrible at first, now it was heartburn. Everything gave her heartburn. Even a plain glass of water gave her heartburn! People said it showed the baby would be born with lots of hair. People also said she looked tired and flushed and asked if she was feeling OK. No she wasn't OK! For a start she was pissed off with 'people'; what did they know about anything! She felt fat, forty and frumpy, and what made it worse was she knew that was exactly how she looked. Gone were the elegantly manicured nails. Gone were the fancy hairstyles - she couldn't hold her arms up long enough to make a French pleat, even if she had the energy to bother. She hadn't seen her feet in months let alone had a pedicure.

There was no pregnancy glow about Caroline; her skin was dry and scaly and her rosy cheeks were the result of constant anger rather than the bloom of health.

Everything irritated her on a daily basis, but today her irritation was overshadowed by agitation.

This was the first art class after the Christmas break. This meant Anthea would be back from Antigua. She would tell the class about her trip, she had lots of gossip to tell everyone apparently. Something about meeting a professional yacht skipper. Caroline didn't want to hear about it. She wanted Antigua to be buried in the past. Maybe Anthea would have jet lag and miss this class then when she came back her news would be old news and nobody would be interested. Caroline was interested, but she still didn't want to hear.

Over the weekend the girls had taken down the Christmas decorations. Each bauble from the tree was wrapped in tissue paper before being stored in a compartmentalised box designed especially for Christmas decorations. Some people collect up all the decorations in one big box and worry about untangling the lights and finding all the ornaments when next Christmas comes around. They might enjoy the hunt each year for the right colour tinsel, finding lights that still worked, and coming across last year's Christmas cards and reminiscing. Ooh look, this one's from Auntie Marge ... hey, this is from the Marshalls, remember them? ... here's the one from John - I wonder how she/they/he is/are doing... But Caroline needed order in her life; she liked to know that everything was ready for the next year, that baubles didn't get lost or broken, that all the special family memento ornaments were safe, that everything was colour coordinated, red green and gold being the traditional colour scheme in the Armstrong household. She still had the little glass teardrop that had been on every tree since she was six years old. There was a wooden tropical fish from Caroline's days in Antigua. Baubles with scenes from the Sistine chapel she and Mark had bought from Vatican City on their honeymoon. Plaster snowflakes painted by the girls when they were in junior school. There was another ornament that had been on every tree since her first Christmas with Mark - a glass cherub.

"Beth, can you pass me the cherub?" said Caroline from her position of overseer on the couch.

"I think I put it in the box already" said Beth with a hint of annoyance.

"Sorry darling, can you see if you can find it?" Caroline had bought the cherub at the airport gift shop. It was to remind her of Steven.

"Found it" cried Beth.

Caroline normally drove a Skoda Citigo automatic; It was great for whizzing around town, and easy to park. Lately though, her bump was so huge she could hardly fit, and she couldn't push the seat back any further yet still reach the steering wheel. Today she was driving Mark's Lexus as he was working from home. It was manual transmission and heavier to drive than her little Skoda, but it was easy to get into and the heated seats were soothing on her tired back. Icy rain lashed against the windscreen, the wipers hardly keeping up with the torrent. As she turned down into the high street, she looked at all the dark figures jostling along the pavement, stooped and leaning into the wind. She was so glad to be warm and dry in the car.

As she headed down the high street on her way to the studio, she saw a flash of red out to the left. Someone on a bike had swung out of a side road veering all over the place on the wet road. A cafe table was being blown by a huge gust of wind and was heading her way - she tried to avoid it, swerving to the right and putting her foot down. The response in the Lexus was much faster than in her little Skoda; the car leapt forward, lurched into the car in front, shoving it sideways and forward at the same time. As if in the one same moment several things happened; the table hit her rear nearside door with a terrific bang, the Lexus ploughed into the rear offside of the car in front with an ominous crunch. The Lexus stalled and stopped; the front and side airbags deployed obscuring all her view, and somewhere somebody screamed.

BACK TO SCHOOL NICK

As Nick drove through the torrential rain towards the cliff road to pick up Fiona, his thoughts turned again to health and hospitals. Fiona had given up driving now and as Martin had dropped out of the class it would have been difficult for her to get to the studio with all the bags and paraphernalia she carried. Nick had offered to pick her up, well aware that Fiona's health was not great and she would lose out on something she obviously enjoyed if she couldn't get to class. But it was more than that.

He recognised that she was having trouble with strength and energy, and like him, she would not admit it. Like him, she would say she was fine when she was obviously not. He was pretty sure her cancer was back. They didn't talk about health - they didn't need to - it was just understood. Fiona was ready and waiting as he pulled up. Nick got out to help with all the art stuff, and they set off back into town.

Nick had a restricted driving license, issued for three years unless his MS symptoms got worse. He didn't expect his situation to change much in three years. Yes, he now walked with a stick, more for balance than support. Yes his left foot was a bit numb, but he had an automatic car now, so it didn't make any difference. Perhaps it was his Army training but it went against the grain to admit, even to himself, that there were things he couldn't do: he just found a way around it.

Someone on a bike suddenly came out of a side road, swerving right in front of the car. It looked like they were having trouble controlling their bicycle on the wet road, and wind was funnelling down between the high buildings, pushing the rider onward.

Nick had excellent reflexes and slammed on the brake just in time, missing the bike by inches. Time slowed down as if he was watching an old cine film of home movies frame by frame.

Nick's right leg went into spasm, his right foot solid and tingling, his right leg straight; an unbendable iron bar. He couldn't feel the pedal anymore and his foot slipped off as it twisted painfully and rigidly. The car started rolling forward again and the slow motion switched to everything happening at once. There was an almighty crash as the car behind slammed into the back of his and the car shot forward towards the bike. He yanked hard on the handbrake to slow the momentum but the car kept on going: he couldn't do anything about it.

The airbags had deployed and Nick couldn't see where he was going. Then he felt it. The sickening crunch as the front wheel rose up and over the fallen bicycle. Someone somewhere screamed.

BACK TO SCHOOL JESS

Jessica was running a little late for art class. She had overslept, missed her bus, had to wait for the next one, and had not had time for breakfast.

When she got to the high street she got out one stop short of the Community Centre and went into a coffee shop for a take away latte and blueberry muffin. The weather was foul; cold, wet and windy, but when it came to a choice between missing breakfast and getting wet, there was really no contest. She couldn't sit for a couple of hours without her morning caffeine hit and her stomach rumbling like a thunderstorm. Last week she had seen the sign that the little cafe at the

Community Centre was closed until the following week for 'necessary refurbishments' and hoped it would mean they were finally going to get a proper coffee machine installed.

Jessica paid for her coffee and muffin and went outside. The coffee shop was on a corner between the high street and a side road down which the wind was howling as it funnelled between the tall buildings. A gust nearly knocked her off her feet. She realised she had made a fundamental mistake with getting a take-away; both hands were needed and she couldn't juggle well enough to reach her umbrella. As another huge gust tore down the road, she abandoned the idea of an umbrella. She put the coffee and muffin on an outside table, unzipped the flap on the collar of her coat and pulled the hood out over her head.

As she was busy trying to wrap herself up against the elements she heard her name called. She looked up to see Anthea on her bicycle coming down the road. She looked like a great red blimp in her waterproof jacket and scarf, all wrapped up with just her eyes showing. Jessica was really pleased to see her, they had become such good friends since they met at the art class. As the youngest of the group they naturally sought out each other's company, but more than that they were such complete opposites, they got on like a house on fire each benefitting from the other's strengths.

Anthea was almost at the corner when several things happened at once. She had turned to shout something to Jessica but her voice was lost in a another huge gust that tore down the street. Jessica's coffee and muffin were blown off the table, then the table itself was blown over and was rolling into the high street. Anthea just managed to swerve out of the way of the table but hadn't been looking where she was going and almost ran into an oncoming car.

Then everything seemed to happen at once. For some reason the oncoming car had swerved and braked hard, then started going forward again straight towards Anthea. She had lost so much momentum that she couldn't keep the bike from wobbling. The wet road didn't help, and the bike collapsed, slamming Anthea onto the ground. The oncoming car was still heading right at her but she was pinned down under the fallen bike and couldn't move.

Jessica watched in horror as the car rode up over the fallen bike and she lost sight of Anthea. Sounds of breaking glass, tearing metal, squealing brakes, then everything stopped. Time stood still. In the seconds it took for everything to come to a standstill there was silence.

Somebody somewhere started screaming, the world was turning again. Jessica realised it was her scream.

CHAPTER 12 - HOSPITALS

AFTERMATH

Caroline felt awful. She kept thinking that if she hadn't felt so anxious about seeing Anthea and the fear of her secret being revealed, she would have been paying more attention and perhaps Anthea wouldn't have been hurt. It almost felt that through malice she had willed Anthea to have the accident.

Fiona had been in the car with Nick and had to go to hospital with broken wrists. Anthea had been taken to hospital in an ambulance and needed an operation Here was she, Caroline; who's worried, anxious, lying, spiteful thoughts had probably caused the accident, and she walked away unscathed. She understood what was meant by survival guilt. She felt guilty as hell.

The art class they had all been travelling to had been cancelled. Nick, Jessica and Caroline sat in shock inside the café. Nick and Caroline had spent ages on their mobile phones calling insurance companies and recovery vehicles. Caroline had phoned Mark; Jessica's parents were away and Nick didn't have any family to call. The ambulance had left, the police had cleared up the scene and gathered information from those involved, including the cafe owners whose pavement table blowing into the road had probably caused the accident. The three friends sat waiting, not wanting to talk. Nick waited for a taxi, Caroline waited for Mark to come and get her, and Jessica waited because she didn't know what else to do.

In the same way we all have to process grief to be able to let it go, they all had to process shock. Eventually they started to talk. Jessica had watched the whole thing happen so could fill in the blanks for the others; it was an accident, nobody to blame, nobody died. Talking was cathartic; the jagged flashes of fear and destruction, the storm waves of panic, became calmer. It would be OK.

Mark pulled up outside the cafe and rushed in looking for Caroline.

"She's fine, she's just gone to the loo" said Jessica when she saw the terror in Mark's face.

Mark collapsed into a chair not realising how stressed and worried he had been on the drive over until that second. He let out a sigh of relief. Mark and Nick briefly talked through what had happened and both agreed it was probably a bona-fide accident from the wind blowing over the cafe table.

"Such an insignificant thing to cause so much damage" said Nick in awe "we were all in the wrong place at the wrong time. Thank heavens it wasn't worse."

Nick's taxi arrived and he offered Jessica a lift so they left Mark alone.

Caroline came down the stairs looking very pale. Mark jumped up and took her in his arms while she sobbed on his shoulder. She loved this man to distraction, he was always there for her, always able to make things right, to pick up the pieces. She sobbed because she felt responsible. She sobbed because she had crashed his car. She sobbed because she was in shock and she sobbed because in the loo she had seen a few spots of blood.

FIONA HOSPITAL

Something was not right. Fiona knew her own body well enough to know something had changed, and it didn't feel right.

Nick is the only one I can trust, she thought. He seems to understand me and cares in a way that Martin doesn't. Perhaps it's his army training that makes him ask me how I am getting on. Oh, everyone asks how I am, and I answer 'I'm fine, same as usual, but fine.' And then having got that charade out of the way, we can resume whatever inane conversation we had been having. But Nick is different - when he asks me how I am, when he looks deeply into my eyes, I know he's really interested - And I know that he knows.

Nick was waiting outside the eatery, waiting for Fiona to be dismissed from her oncologist. He watched the constant stream of staff and visitors come and go. Breakfast smells changing to those of hot soup and pasties as time marched on.

As soon as Fiona joined him Nick knew it was not good news. The oncologist confirmed what they already knew - the cancer was back and had spread to her bones. There was nothing to be done. If it hadn't been for the car accident Fiona wasn't sure she would have even bothered to see the oncologist: she knew in herself the cancer was back.

When the crash happened, Fiona had automatically put her arms out in front to brace herself. When the airbag deployed her hands bent back so suddenly and so painfully she was sure both wrists were broken.

The hospital had insisted on X-rays to determine what kind of fractures they were dealing with, and it was the radiologist who noted the anomalies on the film. Fiona was kept in overnight whilst various tests were done and her oncologist consulted.

Bone metastasis spreading from stomach cancer was not common, and prognosis was never very positive. A matter of months they said.

JESSICA VISITS ANTHEA

Jessica got off the bus at the hospital and went to the gift shop before heading to reception. She bought a teddy with a heart, a box of chocolates and a bunch of flowers. She also carried a get well soon card signed by all the art class.

Anthea had already been in the hospital for a couple of days. When the paramedics cleaned her up, it showed her injuries were mainly superficial. The right side of her face was a mass of scabs from where she had face planted the road. Apparently the nurses in A&E had spent ages picking bits of gravel and dirt out and painting yellow iodine all over to prevent infection, but it was all healing nicely and they didn't think there would be any permanent damage. The masses of blood at the scene had been the result of Anthea nearly biting through her tongue and knocking out three front teeth. That too would heal but she would definitely need a dentist!

The major injury was from being pinned under the bicycle. Her foot and leg were trapped at such an odd angle, she had torn all the ligaments in her knee and had to have an operation to sew them up.

Anthea was sitting up in bed with her left leg resting on a couple of pillows and in a huge cast from toe to thigh.

"Jessica! Thanks so much for coming! Did you bring me tea?" asked Anthea with a laugh.

"Chocolates and flowers - no tea." Jessica smiled. "How are you feeling?"

"Pretty crap really; I'm uncomfortable, can't sleep because I can't turn over, every time I need to pee I have to call the nurse to bring a bedpan, the food is not great - the only saving grace is the food keeps me bunged up so I don't need to poo too!"

"TMI sunshine!" said Jessica grinning "That is an image my mind won't be getting rid of soon enough!"

"Seriously though, it's not too bad, but I am a bit bored and they're not going to release me until I can make it to the loo on my crutches, and walk up 6 stairs." Anthea said glumly.

"I can come again tomorrow if you like? Every day actually now that Christmas is done. I can bring you something to keep you occupied too if you like? Have you got your tablet and charger?"

"I don't have my tablet, but I have my phone and charger. If you could pick it up for me that would be great then I can watch Netflix" said Anthea sounding a bit more positive. "And yes please - come and visit whenever you can - I am starved of gossip and friendly company"

"Done" Said Jessica. "Has anyone else been in?"

"Well actually, Fiona has been in several times. I thought she was a bit cold at first, but she is really caring and sweet! We talk about Art and Life and everything in between. She broke her wrists in the crash so she is out of commission for the time being."

They chatted for a while longer; Anthea telling stories about her Antigua trip and the 'fit' guy she had met there. Jessica talked about her abysmal family Christmas, laughing and joking until it was time for Jessica   to   leave.

Caroline Hospital

Caroline had been very quiet on the drive home after the accident. She was very quiet and withdrawn for days afterwards too. Mark put it down to shock.

In fact Caroline was staying quiet and resting and willing her baby to survive. The spotting she had seen at the cafe after the crash scared her. It continued after she got home. Mark tried to comfort her about the crash, but Caroline had almost forgotten about the accident; she didn't care about it, nobody got seriously hurt.

As she lay in bed or on the couch, her feet on pillows hoping gravity would help, she tried to tell if the baby was moving. Those little butterfly movements that let you know there was a person inside you. Sometimes she thought she felt it.

On Monday the spotting had become a flood. Mark phoned for an ambulance and went with her to the hospital.

When you have spent seven months knowing there is life inside you, you can't help but smile. Being part of a miracle. A feeling of pride and superiority. You talk to your baby, let it know it is loved, make plans for it, sing to it. A unique relationship develops between a mother and child before they even meet. The pain of labour and childbirth is forgotten in an instant as you see this face that hadn't existed before, and although you had never met before, you recognise you have known that face your whole life.

When you know that the baby inside you has died the grief and sadness is overwhelming. Caroline had wanted so much to meet him, to hold him, but she had let him down. She would always love him, but she was scared of giving birth; if she held him, even once, how could she bring herself to give him up. All the while he was still inside, he was still her baby.

At the hospital Caroline was immediately put on a drip to induce labour. Because of her age and how far along she was in the pregnancy she was monitored constantly. It was poignant pain to be in a labour ward while everyone around her was nervous but happily excited. Caroline knew it was Karma; her penance, her punishment.

The consultant explained to her that the car accident, although minor, had caused the placenta to separate from the womb. He explained that as her records indicated she'd had a termination years ago, there might have been uterine scarring that contributed to the instability of the placenta.

Mark stayed with her the whole time. This baby was his and its loss was his also. He liked having a family he could care for and provide for, and he hated being helpless now.

"Do you want to hold him?" asked the midwife gently. Caroline turned away.

"He looks beautiful" said Mark as he stroked his wife's hair. "He just looks like he is sleeping."

Caroline turned back to look at the midwife holding her dead child. With a moment of hesitation she reached out and took him. Tears were running freely down her face. The midwife was talking quietly with Mark about a stillbirth certificate and did they want to name the baby.

Caroline had been tracing a finger over the baby's face, etching it in her memory. His eyelids were almost translucent. She counted his fingers and toes, and without looking up said in a clear strong voice

"His name is Steven."

Caroline was kept in hospital for a couple of days to make sure there were no complications. She had lost a lot of blood and was rather weak, but it was her mental state that was causing concern. Grief counselling was offered along with support for the family, but she just lay there, staring at nothing. Mark visited every day. She didn't want the girls to visit: she couldn't deal with their grief.

On Thursday morning she was ready to be discharged. Mark had promised the doctors he would look after her and make sure she rested. They were sitting together at home in the conservatory, Caroline in a recliner, wrapped in blankets; since the birth she had been constantly cold. There was a growing chasm of silence between them. Mark thought he could deal with his grief by caring for Caroline, but it wasn't working. There was also something odd on his mind.

Chapter 13 - Spring

Valentine's Day

"Morning sunshine" said Jessica as she brought two cups of coffee out onto the decking. It was chilly but crisp and clear. The wind and rain of the previous week had blown itself out and the homes in the holiday park all looked freshly laundered.

Anthea was sitting wrapped up in a blanket with her face up to the winter sun and her leg on a chair.

"This is absolutely beautiful" said Anthea with a smile. "Thanks for letting me stay."

"To be honest, it gets pretty lonely here when my parents go away, so I'm loving it!"

Anthea looked down at her cast. It still looked white and new but decorated now with names and squiggles. It felt like everyone she knew had come to visit her in hospital. Caroline had been in several times bringing flowers or homemade cookies or puzzle books so she wouldn't get bored. At first Anthea thought she was there because of some feeling of guilt and it all felt rather awkward, but after a couple of times they were chatting comfortably and both realised they had made assumptions about each other that were completely wrong. Caroline wasn't the stuck up racist bitch as Anthea had imagined; she was genuinely caring and motherly. Anthea's own mum phoned her every day but she was in Leeds - way too far away to come for a visit since Anthea was only going to be in hospital for a few more days.

The surgeon said that as soon as she learned to use the crutches and could walk to the bathroom by herself, she would be discharged. Because her cast was non-weight-bearing, she needed two crutches and had to hop along on her good leg, swinging the cast through on each step. She could stand and lean on the kitchen counter to make a cup of tea, but she didn't have extra hands to carry it to the next room once she had made it! The surgeon insisted she have someone at home to help.

Anthea lived in a nice flat above a craft shop and the only way she could get upstairs was backwards on her bottom with someone to help carry the weight of her cast. Caroline had offered a spare room, but Jessica suggested staying at the Holiday Park.

"There is a ramp there already that goes up to the decking, and once you are up, everything is on the same level. It's perfect really!" said Jessica. She explained that her parents were off skiing or some such so there was plenty of room.

It had been a good decision.

On Valentine's Day there was always a big do up at the clubhouse. Each year, Jessica spent ages on her hair, make-up and clothes, convinced this would be the night she would meet someone and fall in love. Chairs and tables were moved to the sides of the big room to make a space for dancing. Big red paper hearts and golden stars hung from the ceiling, red and gold confetti sprinkled on every table and a net of red balloons hung from the rafters ready for release at midnight. It looked like a cardiologist's operating theatre gone wrong.

Every year Jessica would sit nursing her vodka cranberry and chat to some of the more elderly residents. She found older people easy to talk to; people her own age caused such anxiety she forgot her native language.

Nobody would ask her to dance or seek out her company or offer to buy her a drink. The older residents would go home around 9:30 and she would be left alone at the table, trying to look self-assured when really she felt lonely and desperate. Every year she watched groups of friends splitting up into couples having intimate moments. The lighting was turned lower, the music got slower and she would leave. She had never seen the balloons drop.

This year, the girls decided to have their own private valentine's party on the deck. Jessica built a fire in the chimenea so they could toast marshmallows. They swaddled themselves in blankets and drank Prosecco, talking and laughing, their breath rising as white vapour in the chill night air. Around midnight they switched to chips and salsa and shots of tequila, and sang songs from their favourite musicals. They talked about old boyfriends, lost loves, and nightmare dates. They laughed about dating apps and terrible profile pictures. As people were leaving the clubhouse they got a lot of looks and smiles.

"Your party sounds way better than ours" said a nice looking guy as he passed "here, have a balloon"

101

and he tied it to the railings around the deck. He kept looking back at Jessica as he walked away. It was the best Valentine she ever had.

FIONA LONELY

Fiona was lonely. Not on the outside where she had plenty of friends and lots of places to go, but on the inside. The special place in the pit of your stomach where you know there is someone there who can feel you, understand you completely. For want of a better word, a soul mate. Some people found their soul mate in marriage, and once it might have been possible for Fiona and Martin, but now there was nothing there except irritation.

The sound of children playing, laughing, squabbling, flowed over the fence from the school at the end of the garden. Soon the bell would ring. Playtime would be over, and the decibel level would drop to a gentle hum until lunch time. She couldn't see the children, the intervening fence and buildings obscured her view, but she could imagine them. Hear them cheering whilst playing rounders, quarrelling over hop-scotch, crying over scraped knees. The innocence and gentleness of daily life for a six year old. She could hardly remember her own childhood, but it must have been fine or she would have had recurring nightmares. She wished she had shown more appreciation to her parents though. Parents seem hard-wired to love you unconditionally, whatever you do, and she could use some of that now.

Fiona wondered whether, if she and Martin had been blessed with children, their lives would have been fuller, more complete, but it wasn't to be and really Fiona had never felt very maternal. In fact having children around her all day would have driven her mad. Listening to them across the fence was wonderful, and not having to be responsible for them made it even sweeter.

The weather in the spring was blissful - the South of England enjoying a mini heat wave; for the time of year it was gorgeous. Sitting under the apple tree having her morning coffee, Fiona watched the birds flitting from branch to branch, chattering with each other, always busy, always moving. The blossom was just forming on the tree; tiny buds of green and pinky white. It would be a huge crop this year. Every year she had promised herself that she would pick the apples before they dropped. There were just so many of them. Dropping with soft thuds on the grass to lie there; pecked by birds, invaded by bugs, trampled by boots, until they were a useless rotting soggy mess that had to be cleared and thrown on the compost heap before the man could cut the grass. Every year she promised herself she would make apple sauce, crumble, stewed apples and fill up the freezer, but every year life got in the way and the garden became littered with rotting fruit, a feast only for wasps.

This year Fiona felt guilt and sadness because the Universe had provided such a wonderful tree that marked the seasons so clearly, that gave her shade and beauty, yet she had squandered its fruit. She knew, as she looked at the myriad of tiny buds, the smallest branches reaching out to the sun, that she wouldn't be around when the apples came.

All was quiet again across the fence and birdsong filled the void. So many different types that she didn't recognise. Again she felt guilt and sadness. Guilt that she had not taken the time and effort to learn more about the beautiful world outside her back door, and sad because now it was probably too late.

She didn't want to die alone. She wanted someone to sit quietly with her, hold her hand, watch the blossom grow, tell her they would stay with her, tell her not to be scared.

THE TRUTH WILL OUT

It had been weeks since Caroline had been discharged from hospital but her grief was still as raw as ever it had been. Nothing Mark did seemed to help; she had withdrawn from everyone and everything, sitting in the conservatory, staring at nothing. Mark brought her a cup of tea and took the seat opposite.

"There is something that has been bothering me." he started softly and a little fearfully "The girls wanted to know why you named the baby Steven when you already have a son called Steven?"

Caroline's reaction was surprising. It was the first time she had shown any animation since the tragedy. She took a steadying breath; she always knew this day would come.

"Steven doesn't exist." she said flatly

"What do you mean?" Mark looked totally confused "of course he exists! You talk to him every week! ... I don't understand."

"It means I made him up".

"what?"

"It means I was pregnant ... then I had an abortion".

"WHAT!" shouted Mark "Why? When?"

In a very plain voice, devoid of any emotion, she told him about Steve and about Antigua. About how the love of her life had been horrified when she fell pregnant; how Steve convinced her that if they were to carry on in the yacht charter business she should get an abortion, how he offered to pay. She had wanted that baby. It had been made from love. She had worried that she wouldn't love the child as much as she loved Steve. She told Mark how all those years ago in the Caribbean she had walked into the clinic in St John's on her own, had paid with her own money, had felt the cold empty loss when the procedure was over, and had left alone.

Mark was silent for a long time. He stood up to fix himself a drink and went out into the garden without a word. Caroline could see him on one of the lawn chairs, his shoulders shaking like he was sobbing. Still Caroline could not feel. She was remembering how it all happened, how it all felt when she got back to the marina. Steve was drinking in the bar with a stewardess from another yacht and thoughtlessly asked Caroline if she had a successful visit to town. The grief inside her burned. What had been love turned to hate; she wanted to claw at him, to bite and hit and gouge until he was as bloody a mess as her aborted child. She couldn't believe that she had done such a terrible thing, done it for Steve because she loved him so much, and she couldn't believe Steve was so heartless and selfish not to feel her pain. Then she realized she could believe it and hated herself for not seeing it before and for being so weak. For a few days she went about her life as if nothing had happened - nobody knew what she had done, but she was too different. She had not a shred of emotion or compassion, she hated herself and didn't know where to turn. On Wednesday night when Steve was drinking beer and laughing in the cockpit with friends, she slipped into their cabin and took money from the safe. She called British Airways and booked a seat on the flight out the next day. In the morning she told Steve she was going to St. John's to get provisions. In her handbag she had her passport and money. She took the bus into town, then a taxi to the airport. She had no idea what she was going to do when she got back to UK, she just knew she had to get out of there.

Mark came back inside, his eyes red and swollen.

"Why did you do it? Why did you lie?"

"I thought about that baby that never was" she said and her voice got softer as she thought of that missing family. "I thought about him every day; I imagined him growing up, how old he would be now. Then one day I found a picture frame in a camera shop, the boy in the picture looked just like I expected my son to grow up looking like…." her voice tailed off.

"You lied to me?" whispered Mark.

"Yes"

"I still don't understand Why?" said Mark without comprehension.

She didn't answer for a while and then said "Nobody knew about the baby, not even that it had existed, however briefly, but he was real to me."

Anger was bubbling up inside him; anger at being lied to, anger for living that lie for years, for involving the whole family. Anger that she hadn't trusted him with the truth before they married, or after, or when they had children, or at any time in their marriage before now! He looked at her in horror as if she had just killed her whole family and didn't care.

The truth was she really did care and she wished she had never lied to Mark and to the girls, but she was completely empty. The imaginary Steven and the stillborn Steven had merged in her mind as if the car accident had caused a disturbance in the space-time continuum. She had lost both her sons and had no-one to blame but herself.

That night Mark insisted she tell the girls the whole story. They all sat at the kitchen table. Caroline the accused, facing all three victims as if in a courtroom. Confession.

The girls were distraught. They had always bragged their mum was the best; a real stay at home mother who made cookies. Helped both with homework and hormones, totally dependable. But now they knew she had lied to them; that every birthday card from Steven had been a trick, that Caroline herself had written the emails, that she had spent hours creating Photoshop pictures of their half-brother. They felt cheated and conned. How could anyone deceive their own family for years?

Caroline didn't try to justify her actions, she was resigned to her fate, to her punishment. She was being fed to the lions and she deserved it. She remained in the kitchen while her family railed at her. She stayed there while Mark phoned his sister to arrange for himself and the girls to stay for a few days. Caroline stayed at the kitchen table as her family packed their bags and left the house. She was alone.

The kitchen clock ticked loudly, marking time. She wanted time to stop, perhaps go backwards. She didn't feel anything. Her emotions were numb. Eventually, long after it had gone dark, she made her way to the lounge and curled up on the couch pulling her blanket over her head and shutting out the world.

CHAPTER 14 - SUMMER TERM

SUMMER TERM

Jessica was still modelling for the Life Drawing class and Nick was still teaching, but the energy seemed to have left the class. Everything was different. There was a darkness in the air that no amount of light could dispel.

Caroline had not been back to the class since the accident although she sometimes met up with the others at coffee break, just to stay in touch. When she met with the art class in the newly upgraded coffee shop, she looked forward to connecting with people again, but once she was there, she couldn't find any common ground and wanted to be left alone. She also carried a weight of guilt that she might have caused the accident; she felt the need to constantly apologise to Anthea for any harm done, and to the rest of the class because she lied. It didn't make any difference that nobody blamed her, that they wanted her to stop apologising, in essence she was apologising from herself to herself.

Home life for Caroline was difficult; her daughters had returned home so they could get back to school. On the surface it looked as if everything was back to normal. They all acted appropriately when in public together, but in private the girls kept their distance from their mother. No more family nights. Mark had also returned home. He too kept his distance. She wanted to be punished, to be whipped or stoned, or just screamed at; she wanted to atone but she couldn't break through the iron curtain that divided her from her family. She found solace in a wine glass. When she wasn't drinking herself into oblivion, she would drive around aimlessly, wanting to connect with people yet wanting to be on her own at the same time.

Nick brought Fiona in each week, but her struggles with pain were getting worse. She was getting very thin because she couldn't swallow food easily. Nick spent a lot of time at Fiona's house keeping her company, sometimes just sitting together peacefully looking out over the water to the Isle of Wight. Fiona often invited Caroline to visit too, but knowing Fiona's days were numbered and that however bad her own life was, at least it was life, Caroline felt too guilty to visit.

June 21st, the longest day of the year; officially the start of summer in the Northern hemisphere. Fiona used to hate this date; it meant that the days would turn a tiny bit shorter, that the year was dying. She knew that for her it was the last Summer Solstice she would ever see. As she was staring at the view along the cliff tops, she heard car tyres crunching on the driveway. For a horrible moment she thought it was Martin come back to drain her energy, and was glad Nick was close by making cups of tea, then she heard Caroline's voice.

"Look who I found on the doorstep." said Nick as he brought in the tea. Caroline came into the room tentatively; she and Fiona had never been close friends, but Fiona looked delighted to see her. Nick went back to the kitchen for another cup whilst Caroline sat in a recliner opposite Fiona.

They talked for a while about nothing in particular; the weather, the fact the English always talk about the weather, but it was hard to think of subjects that didn't project a future Fiona could never be part of. Nick left to go and buy biscuits and there was a pregnant pause.

"One thing about dying - you really learn to value time." said Fiona.

Caroline was taken aback by such a direct statement, and by Fiona's pragmatic approach to the subject of dying.

"I spent countless years living a lie; a marriage with someone I stopped loving, grief for children I never had, loneliness and broken hearts." said Fiona, "we are not so different you and I."

Tears welled up in Caroline; compassion, sadness and guilt. This time the guilt was for being selfish. Feeling sorry for herself in the company of Fiona who faced a bleaker future than herself.

"I am so so sorry." tears were falling freely now "I don't know what to say".

"You need to say you are sorry and mean it, but to yourself. You need to forgive yourself." said Fiona. "You have the most precious gift of all, the gift of time; time to grieve, time to forgive but not forget".

Fiona looked back at her special view dry eyed while Caroline sobbed in the background.

"Everything takes time" she said quietly "even dying".

Fiona feebly hoped Caroline would be able to turn her life around; hoped that she would break the circle of guilt and constant regret. It took impending death to make one understand the stupidity and banality of family rows and lies. If she gave nothing else, Fiona hoped she had given Caroline a way back to her family.

By the time Caroline had left, Fiona was emotionally drained, in terrible pain and couldn't focus on anything. She would wait for Nick to come back and he would get some of her drugs. Her life had reduced to periods of unbearable agony followed by fatigue and brain fog. It takes time to die; she wondered how much longer she had to wait.

NICK

When Nick found Fiona a little while later, he could tell the time had come to go to the hospice. He lifted her up from the floor where she'd slid off the chair; she was so fragile, like a baby bird. Caring for Fiona, he had been useful, felt needed. He had felt needed in his marriage and he knew Jenny had felt safe and cherished with him. When the MS switched the dynamics so completely, neither of them could deal with it. He knew now what he wanted. As much as he enjoyed art, it had begun to feel like rather a frivolous pastime. He needed to re-evaluate his own life, make a fresh start; he would stay with Fiona to the end, but then he would leave. He had been approached by the charity Help for Heroes and offered a volunteer role at Tedworth House

Recovery Centre. He knew about the place from his Army days. A facility to rehabilitate ex- military with medical disabilities or PTSD and bring them back into society, and he would use art therapy to do it. More than being useful and needed, Tedworth House was not that far from Oxford, and Oxford was where Jenny was ... For now though, he was committed to Fiona.

Martin had disappeared into an alcoholic haze; no longer pretending to be a doting husband. They were not even sure where Martin was living. Fiona scarcely gave him a passing thought. Nick had been staying in the spare room for the last week. Fiona had told him everything he might need to know; where to find her birth certificate, Will, bank account details, relatives who might want to come to the funeral, where she wanted to be cremated, and where to scatter her ashes. Fiona said all this in an unemotional voice; she'd had time enough to think things through, and rehearsed what she needed to say enough times to enable her to relate it without feeling.

When the hospice transport arrived, Fiona was back in her recliner looking at her favourite view. There were tears in her eyes as she was transferred into a wheelchair and loaded onto the ambulance. Nick got in beside her and held her hand. She did not give a backward glance.

"I wish I could get my hands free". Fiona was scratching around the cannula attached to the back of her hand.

"I wish lots of things" said Nick gently.

"I'm so tired, but it's impossible to sleep with all the noise going on around here. I have nightmares."

"Tell me what you dream about?"

"Beep beep click bump hiss, bump hiss, all day long … all night long" Fiona stared at a spot on the ceiling "and the machines are not in sync so it sounds like an orchestra constantly tuning up and never getting to start the symphony".

"What are you talking about?" Nick was completely stumped. Fiona drifted between periods of reality where her thoughts were structured and logical, followed by much longer periods of drug addled quiescence - not quite asleep, not quite dead.

"My dream! In my dream, I am paralysed, immobile in an iron lung, in a ward full of iron lungs. I saw a photo once of a hospital ward during a polio epidemic in the fifties" Fiona went quiet, seeing again the adults and children, all stuck in row after row of huge machines with just their heads sticking out. Like a beehive nursery and all the pupae waiting to be fed and waiting … waiting.

"I am so sorry, that's awful"

"Don't be sorry, it is what it is. I think being hooked up to all these monitors, unable to move, beep click bump hiss, it's all doing my head in."

"I wish there was something I could do."

"Get me home?"

"Is that what you want?"

"I want to not be dying …"

Fiona closed her eyes and was quiet for a while. Nick sat and listened to her breathing and the background beep click bump hiss of the monitors.

"I want to go home." Fiona's voice made him jump - he thought she was asleep. "I want to see the sands at Alum Bay and hear the waves suck and hiss on the pebbles."

"Are you sure?" he asked quietly

"Yes. I'm sure."

It had taken more than a little effort to arrange things. The hospice was not eager to release anyone without a good deal of precautions and contingencies, but the nature of the beast is always to give palliative care and help someone in whatever way was possible. Nick was given custodial care of her medication and at Fiona's request, the hospice arranged for a solicitor to visit and prepare all the necessary paperwork. With time running out for Fiona, everything was prepped and ready, and by Friday, the ambulance was there to take her home.

Fiona died at home in her own bed, propped up with pillows so she could see the view she loved so much. Nick was with her the whole time.

CHAPTER 15 - FUNERALS

FIONA R.I.P.

The funeral service was held at a non-denominational chapel of rest at the crematorium. Nick wanted to be a pall bearer, but his balance and leg might have caused a catastrophe, so he settled for talking a little about Fiona.

"I met Fiona at a life drawing class in Horton Regis. She was a strong woman with an amazing amount of talent, and a huge amount of love." he said. "She used to talk about how the art class was such an inspiration both for her art and for life - she connected with people she probably wouldn't have met under different circumstances." He talked about her love of painting, of music, of literature.

Anthea and Jessica sat next to each other near the front, sniffing and blowing, with Caroline sitting just behind. Although they had known each other for such a short time the connection between them all was strong. So much had happened to change all their lives.

Nick invited anyone who wanted to put a memento on the coffin to come and do so. Jessica went up and put a paint brush on the coffin; Anthea slipped a card she had written under the flowers; Caroline took out of her pocket the glass cherub Christmas ornament she had bought to remind her of Steven so many years ago, it was time for her to let go.

When Caroline returned to her seat she saw that Mark was sitting at the back. He had slipped in unnoticed to pay his respects. She looked at him with such longing, such pleading, and such love that his heart went out to her.

Everyone stood whilst the coffin was lowered out of sight. Barbra Streisand sang "The Way We Were" while they all processed outside to view the flowers and to cry and hug. Caroline was sobbing silently, this funeral was for Fiona but it was also saying goodbye to the sons that might have been. She felt, rather than saw, Mark coming up behind her. He took her hand and she spun round and gave a guttural sob and folded herself into his arms. "I'm sorry. I'm so very sorry." she stammered between sobs. Mark said nothing, just held her and stroked her hair.

Nick had arranged for a small wake at a local pub; the members of the art class sat together reminiscing about things they had shared. Laughing about Patrick and his ink splodges and Nick and his rope, and the awful instant coffee they served in the community centre cafe. Mark sat next to Caroline, continuing to hold her hand. She understood this meant he was coming back to her; maybe it wouldn't be the same, maybe he could never trust her again, but maybe it was enough for now.

EPILOGUE

ANTHEA STORY

I was six when my father left us. It had never been a good marriage, they had only married because mum was pregnant, but they weren't really compatible. Mum liked the bohemian lifestyle; art and literature and free expression. Byron, my dad, liked dinner on the table at 6pm and left the domestics alone. Even though we didn't live together anymore, we kept in touch and he still supported me.

I was sixteen when mum married again. Another West Indian, this time from Jamaica. He and I didn't get along. He smoked weed from morning 'til night and he kept leering at me. I had left secondary school and took an extended diploma in Art and Design at the Leeds Art University. This led to my BA and then to my Master's degree. Leeds is my home town so I didn't need to be resident at the University, but I chose to move out from home where life was getting complicated. Mum and Don had gravitated from weed to crack; they were permanently stoned or drunk or both, and Don was in the habit of creeping up behind me and putting his hand on my bottom.

The night it happened I had been home for the weekly family dinner. Mum was stoned and passed out in her armchair. Don was stoned and drunk but still upright and swaying in time to Bob Marley. I was standing by the bookcase when he came up behind me.

He put his hands on the bookcase either side of me, pinning me to it, pushing his groin into me. I couldn't move. Why couldn't I move? Why wasn't I kicking and screaming. I was frozen to the spot and didn't understand. I remember the sweet sickly smell of his rum sodden breath on the back of my neck. I remember his hands feeling around under my top, pushing my bra up so the underwires squeezed my breast and dug into my skin. I remember his hands kneading my breasts brutally. I remember wondering why my mum didn't save me, didn't rescue me, didn't protect me.

I spent another year at University but never went back to the house. I don't think my mum noticed. I don't think anyone noticed a change in me either; I started wearing trackies or jeans, never skirts where wandering hands could immigrate. I stopped wearing low cut tops and make up and heels. I stopped wearing anything that had anything to do with showing I was female.

When I completed my Masters in Art and Graphic Design I left Leeds. I tried to explain to mum why I was going, but she wouldn't hear a bad word said against Don. I couldn't get through to her in her drug addled state and she didn't seem that interested in what I was doing, only where her next fix was coming from.

I was in London for a while before I came to Horton Regis. I got a job at an art gallery; it was a good job but like Leeds the big city was lonely and anonymous. I felt I was always looking round corners and checking I wasn't being followed, so I moved down here. I now work part time as an art therapist with autistic children.

I joined the life drawing class because I love life drawing, but also I hoped to meet people. I had been really lonely since I arrived down South, there's not much scope for social connections in my job.

Meeting Fiona was a real bonus. I knew her work from my time in the London gallery but had never met her. She seemed such a cold fish at first, and the way she treated her husband was terrible. Then Martin started trying to flirt with me; touching my arm, getting too close. Fiona saw it but didn't seem to care. I tried to keep my distance but he was relentless. It was Don all over again. After a while I had to say something so I cornered Fiona and asked her to tell Martin to keep away from me. That's when it started really. Fiona was so protective of me, so unlike my mother who just let Don get on with it. Whatever Fiona said to her husband it worked. He didn't come near me again.

I told her all about working in the gallery in London and knowing about her work. She invited me to her home and I saw her amazing view and recognised the landscape that I had seen in her paintings. We used to spend long afternoons discussing art and history and literature. I knew she was sick but I didn't know how bad it was until the accident. She visited me every day in hospital. She told me then that the cancer had spread to her bones.

When I came out of hospital and was staying with Jessica, she came over and kept me company nearly every day. She knew she only had a few months, but we still talked about the future. She was always keen to hear about my dreams and plans, and we would make imaginary plans for what we would do in the future. We both knew there wasn't going to be a future, but we had fun planning it anyway.

Fiona said she felt a connection with me, like I did with her. She said I was like her in many ways and that I was the daughter she never had. To be honest, Fiona has been more of a mother to me than my own mum. It's just so sad to try and fit a lifetime into a few short months.

Jessica knew how close I was with Fiona, as did Nick, but for some reason it was never mentioned to others. I don't really understand why that was, but neither Fiona or I ever mentioned it at life class.

When Fiona went into Ashaven I visited her every day. She was so pragmatic about her position and she appreciated everything that was being done for her, but she really missed her muse; her view. Nick was brilliant throughout. He is really going to miss Fiona; I think that is why he is leaving Horton Regis, too many memories, too many empty spaces.

Fiona has named me beneficiary in her will. She left me a letter too…

My dearest Anthea. If you are reading this you know I am gone, but I will always be with you in spirit and watch over you.

I have wondered for a long time what it would have been like to have children, and I think that is why God gave me you. You have shown me how to be a parent, and I could not be prouder of you.

The most precious gift I could ask for is time; time to spend learning more about what makes us tick, time to spend planning our futures and dreams. Time is something I cannot give you, but hopefully I can give you your dreams.

With the proceeds of this house, I hope you will realise your dream of owning a gallery. All my paintings are coming to you too, so you will be able to start with a full gallery from day one.

I say all my paintings, but I want you to give the blue landscape to Jessica. It was from our very first class and it rightfully belongs to her ...

I didn't read any further because it is all too raw, but I have kept the letter to read at a later date when I can cope with it. A year ago the people in the art class didn't know each other existed, now there's an invisible bond that has very little to do with art and everything to do with life.

Jessica has moved into the flat with me so she is now free of her toxic parents. It's true what they say about being able to choose your friends but not your family. First thing Jess did when she moved in was hang her blue landscape on the wall. When we have visitors they often comment on the lovely landscape and we can't help but smile because they have no idea it was actually a picture of Jess in the nude!

We are looking at premises at the moment. I say we because Jess and I have decided to join forces; if we get a place big enough to put a little cafe in, Jess will run that whilst I run the gallery. We reckon we have a much better chance of meeting smart rich guys there than we would at the holiday park.

"If a train doesn't stop at your station, it wasn't your train" (Marianne Williamson)

BUT - if the train stops, climb aboard, enjoy the ride, you get to choose the destination. Life is too long to be living a life you hate. (Anthea Spencer) ◎

THE END

Printed in Great Britain
by Amazon